Ruler of All That He Sees . . .

Hundreds of Chinese were falling into the streets. Every fifth bullet was hollow-nosed, and expanded on impact to tear off an arm or a leg, or to blow a hole through a man's gut that would accommodate a football.

The upward tilt of the guns sent great chunks of bleeding meat and tripe flying skyward. The streets were spattered with a rain of blood and meat and guts and spent lead.

Countless, perhaps more than a thousand, Chinese were dead, and another thousand or so were dying in moaning agony all around the legation bastion.

*The Casca series
by Barry Sadler*

CASCA:

THE CURSED

BARRY SADLER #18

JOVE BOOKS, NEW YORK

CASCA #18: THE CURSED

A Jove Book / published by arrangement with
the author

PRINTING HISTORY
Jove edition / August 1987

ISBN: 0-515-09109-X

CHAPTER ONE

The old Hakka peasant, Deng Ziyang, brought his two-wheeled cart to a halt against a mud wall beside the dusty road. He looked around cautiously, then spoke softly to the load of cut grass and bullock manure that he was hauling.

"Honorable barbarian, Cas-Ca Sho, we have arrived at Shou-Chang. Please to get out of cart quickly and invisibly, as my head will be forfeit if you are seen."

The ill-smelling load moved slightly, and a hand and a face appeared amongst the grass and cow dung. The face looked unhappily back down the long dirt road that had jolted him the thirty miles from the river port of Tsungkow. It was there he had met the old man and contracted with him for the ride to Shou-Chang.

He had introduced himself as Casca, but the Chinese made two words of it, and, taking it for his surname, demanded another. Casca had recalled his first visit to China in the second century and had supplied "Sho"—long life.

"Can I enter this building in safety, honorable one?" the passenger asked the old man.

"Yes, please," the Chinese replied. "Please hurry to enter humble store of my eldest daughter and worthless

1

son-in-law. It is three more days yet to market day, and for that time this little village will be very quiet.''

From where he crouched, under the load of manure, Casca appraised the small village as he waited for an approaching leper to pass the cart.

The daughter's store was one of the first buildings in the town, a small hut of mud brick with a thatch roof. A broken sign hanging from the wall proclaimed its wares, which seemed to consist only of rice and rice flour. Beyond it Casca could see the huge, wooden gates hanging open from the stone wall that surrounded Shou-Chang. Several beggars, blind and lame, sat in the road, leaning against the gates, their hands stretched out toward the nonexistent traffic on this nonmarket day. A small boy and two smaller girls came behind the leper, the boy carrying two large buckets of water on a wooden yoke around his neck, the girls each with a pitcher of water on their heads.

"Now?" he whispered as the last girl passed.

"Now," hissed the Chinese, and Casca slid from the cart and moved quickly to the doorway opening in the mud wall. He didn't stop to glance down into the village, but kept moving until he was in a dark corner of the store farthest from the door.

"Ju Songzhen," the old man called from behind him, and in answer a Chinese woman appeared from the back of the store. "Make this honorable barbarian welcome in your unworthy house. He comes on important business, but none must know of his being here."

The woman answered in a dialect that Casca could not understand, but he guessed her protest easily enough. Visitors were rare in any Chinese village, and, thus, were a matter of interest for everybody, and especially for the village headman and his assistants. A barbarian visitor was an object of deep suspicion, and the concealment of such a person could easily result in a family's ruin.

Casca seated himself on a low wooden stool, the only furniture in the store other than a crude wooden counter surrounded by a number of partially empty sacks. His reluctant hostess and her father argued, the woman screeching shrilly in the local dialect, the man answering her in Cantonese for Casca's benefit. It quickly became clear that all of the woman's protestations were being met by the old man's obstinate reference to his daughter's poverty; the worthlessness of her husband; and the golden opportunity that Tai-Tsu Yeh, the benevolent spirit of the mountains, had provided in the shape of this barbarian who had paid so generously for his ride from Tsungkow, and who would pay her even more generously for just a few nights' accommodation, and a few small meals.

And, the old woman repeatedly stressed, her silence.

Casca also heard repeated reference to the Hakka code of hospitality and the merit to be acquired in the eyes of the gods through taking care of strangers in their need.

In considerable relief, Casca realized that the old man was winning the argument, and eventually the woman turned to him.

To his surprise, now that she had accepted the situation, she spoke civilly, even pleasantly, and in Cantonese.

"Welcome to our insignificant abode, honorable barbarian. The chief of this humble family is absent at present. He is about his urgent breadwinning activities, but I shall send for him and he will make you decently welcome."

She reverted to the high-pitched dialect shriek, shouting toward the rear of the store where Casca could see two small heads almost hidden behind a sack curtain. In response two small children came scurrying and ran across the store and into the street. The woman moved to the back of the store and busied herself by the small fire with a kettle and a teapot, which she brought quickly to the two men, together with cups and a small plate of rice cakes.

"Ju Liqun will be here presently," the old man said, "just as soon as his long-suffering children can drag him away from his disgraceful debauchery." He lapsed into silence and sipped at his tea.

From where he sat, Casca could see a slice of the village street through the open doorway. The street curved and twisted its way through the town, as did all Chinese streets, no matter what the terrain. Evil spirits like to travel in straight lines. All the buildings seemed to be of bricks made from mud and straw. Barefoot people came and went, their noses running in the bitter mountain cold. Most were carrying heavy loads on the wooden yokes or on their heads, or were pulling the clumsy two-wheeled carts like the one on which he had arrived from Tsungkow.

On the far side of a small village square he could see a porticoed temple, with more beggars sitting on its lowest steps, while sleek, plump Buddhist priests in saffron robes ambled about its broad stone plaza. Where the crumbling street twisted beyond the temple he glimpsed an old peasant plodding behind a plow pulled by a water buffalo, and another whose plow was pulled by a woman. Along the street there passed an occasional loaded ass or horse, or an ox cart; once, Casca caught a glimpse of a two-humped camel.

Casca sipped at his tea and reflected on his long journey from the British compound in Hong Kong that had caused him to be here in the first place. An overnight coastal steamer had carried him in comparative luxury north to Swatow. Then a long, dirty train ride had taken him to Chaochow on the Han River. From there he had ridden for two days on a riverboat, almost enjoying the silent motion of the single-masted sampan as they made their way through the dense river traffic of other sampans, rafts, canoes, and the occasional high-pooped junk. Casca liked to watch the husband-and-wife crew rowing with their rhythmic, dancelike steps, outer legs moving back and forth in a sort of stationary ballet, the oars whipping the water like the fins of some great fish.

The boat people, whose craft went back in time beyond the gondoliers of Venice, the boat men of the Volga, or the seagoing Vikings, were outcasts on shore, illiterates who were born to live, work, and die on their boats. Yet they were a capable and proud people in their closed world of peaceful industry.

As Casca dwelled on these strong yet gentle people, his own reasons for being here came sharply into focus.

CHAPTER TWO

It was the Year of the Boar, 2553 in the Chinese calendar, 1899 in the calendar used by the English, and Sergeant Cassius Longman of Her Majesty's Forty-second Foot Regiment was anything but happy with the assignment he had been given by the British consul in Hong Kong.

Casca had come to China en route from the Americas for Calcutta, where he had hopes of finding service in the British East India Company, training native troops in the use of a newly developed breech-loading musket.

Ashore in Hong Kong, he had become embroiled in a poker game. He had quickly discerned that he had no chance of winning, due to the phenomenal luck enjoyed by two British China Company sergeants who had arrived on the same boat as Casca. One or the other of them seemed to win almost every pot.

Casca allowed the sergeants to cheat just long enough to be certain of what was happening, then he cut his losses and withdrew to wait in a bar across the street until the game ended and the two sergeants set out for their barracks.

When they saw Casca lurching drunkenly toward them in a narrow, twisting alley they were surprised, but not unduly concerned. They feigned injured innocence when he accused them of cheating, and outraged annoyance when he demanded recompense of double his losses.

Sublimely confident of their own ability to beat any three or four men they might encounter, even if they were all Casca's size, they told him to hop it.

Then they started to move so fast Casca had little choice about what happened next.

He saw the quick glance exchanged between the two cheats as they realized that this sucker had still more money and that they could get it. They moved slightly apart, to be able to attack Casa from both sides.

Casca made as if to run, and the closer of the two men lunged for him so that he was badly off-balance as Casca swung around to grab him with both hands and use his own momentum to ram him hard against the stone wall. The force of their combined weights broke his skull like an eggshell. As Casca let the man fall, he turned. The second sergeant aimed a kick at his groin, but Casca moved back, getting his hand under the sergeant's heel, and lifted until the man crashed heavily to the cobblestones.

Casca was on him in an instant, hammering his head into the stones. A few more moments and the fight was quite over, and Casca had stripped and emptied the pockets of both corpses. Another few minutes and two more bodies were added to the harbor's nightly collection of rubbish.

Casca had good reason to be pleased with his take. In place of the five English pounds that he had lost he now had more than a hundred, along with a silver-handled knife and a crocodile-skin wallet.

Inside the wallet he found a British army pay book, together with a letter of posting from the British China Company, which said that the bearer was to report to the Forty-second Foot Regiment barracks on the day after his arrival in Hong Kong, where he was to put himself under the orders of the officers of Her Britannic Majesty, by the Grace of God of the United Kingdom of Great Britain and Ireland and of the British Dominions beyond the Seas, Queen, Defender of the Faith, Empress of India.

"Quite a title," Casca mused, "and one more to add."

Amongst colonial professionals it was held certain that Victoria would be declared "Empress of China" at the London celebrations to mark the turn of the century.

Dawn found Casca at the barracks, where he had little difficulty in reproducing the dead man's signature and so identified himself as Sergeant Cassius Longman, a name close enough to Casca Longinus for him to feel comfortable with it. The other sergeant's name, Henry Arnsworth, didn't seem to be made for him.

It turned out that Sergeant Longman was to be a drill instructor. As the British China Company didn't use native troops, his duties were punitive drilling of men charged with minor discipline infractions, and the early-morning parades. He quickly picked up the complicated British army drill from the mercenaries under his control, and was soon quite comfortable in his little hut in the sergeants' barracks.

But this state of well-being was not to last very long. And Casca had no choice but to blame it all on one Lieutenant Marshman.

One night the drunken lieutenant had strangled a whore in a back-alley cathouse, an offense that just might have eventually resulted in some sort of punishment, possibly even a hanging. But she had been Casca's favorite, almost his private whore, and he had been fond of her little brother, and of her two tiny children; so, he had appointed himself both judge and executioner.

The end result found Casca unhappily exchanging the drill square for the assignment he had been given by the British consul.

But then, he was even more unhappy about the only alternative he had been offered—a formal hanging in the Hong Kong military prison. Her Majesty's government frowned severely upon sergeants who killed lieutenants, no matter how much the officer might deserve killing.

CHAPTER THREE

Lieutenant Marshman had arrived in China only a few weeks earlier, having sought service in the Far East because of the tales he had heard of the beautiful, lascivious women, their ready inclination to perversion, and their extreme poverty, which made them available as slaves to any whim of any man.

He had been profoundly disappointed with what he found. The debased whores of the shantytown red-light district that had grown around the outer perimeter of the British army barracks were a far cry from the cultured courtesans described by Marco Polo and other visitors to the East who had recorded their travels for the information—or titillation—of European readers.

What exotic charms the women did possess were wasted on the Englishman. His ideal of feminine beauty was a fantasy creature based upon the artistocratic English rose, but without the excessively long nose or the prominent teeth and with the peaches-and-cream complexion and ample bosom of a country milkmaid. This figment of a sex-starved imagination had huge, round, blue eyes, and thick blond hair that fell in cascades to her rump. And in lieu of the real-life aristocrat's aloof frigidity, this ideal woman was permanently consumed with a passion to receive into her body in every possible way, and in an endless ecstasy of excitement, the tiny member of this fat, flabby, inbred younger son of a fast-failing third-rate aristocratic family.

Fei Jiyun had been especially disappointing. Marshman was revolted by everything about her except the price. The epicanthic fold that hooded her almond eyes repelled him even more than the black depths of their loveliness. Her body was slight and muscular; her tiny breasts not even as large as his own; her buttocks so slim that he could hold both in one of his huge, fat hands while with the other he tried desperately to fit his half-erect piece of meat into the tight little slit between Jiyun's legs.

Fei Jiyun did her best to help him, spreading her legs wide, nibbling at his ears and neck, fondling his scrotum. But his lack of any real desire for this woman, together with his advanced state of drunkenness, defeated all their joint efforts.

His failure to enter her before he ejaculated infuriated him, and he cuffed the cowering girl unmercifully about the head, squeaking at her in English every term of abuse he could lay his tongue to.

"Filthy slut," he rasped. "Dirty rotten useless thing. Slant-eyed harlot. Titless fucking dwarf. Not a woman at all, just an ugly yellow thing."

In the next room Fei Qili tried to stop his ears to the lieutenant's curses, the sound of his blows, the whimpering of his sister. But as the frustrated lecher's fury grew, his blows fell more and more heavily, and Jiyun's cries turned to despairing moans. Qili snatched up a small stool, the only solid object in his room, and hurled himself upon the naked white man's back, striking him several times on the head before the leg he was holding came loose and the stool went flying to leave the small boy confronting the now thoroughly enraged lieutenant.

Marshman's huge fists smashed the boy's head from side to side. Fei Jiyun clung to Marshman's back, her arms around his thick waist, begging him to stop. At the same time she was bewailing Qili's interference.

"Stupid little boy," she cried at him, "you know you must never fight with any barbarian, no matter what. Better always that one of us suffer rather that two."

But the boy had no further interest in her remonstrations, nor in anything else. He was quite unconscious, Marshman holding his inert body with one great hand while the other dealt blow after blow to the loosely flopping head.

For the first time since he had come to Asia, Marshman was enjoying himself. The blood squirting from the boy's smashed nose aroused him to greater frenzy. The girl was now on her knees on the floor behind him, her arms around his thighs, her fluttering hands clutching him here and there, frequently chancing upon his penis, which was now truly erect for perhaps the first time in his life.

He let the boy's slack body fall to the floor and turned on Fei Jiyun, knocking her to the floor and falling on top of her, ramming himself into her.

She screamed as he forced his way through her unready vaginal opening and screamed again as he thrust frantically into the depths of her body.

"Scream, do you? You filthy prostitute. Don't you scream at me."

He clamped his big hands around her throat and shook her like a rag doll.

Fei Jiyun's pelvis and thighs jerked in a response spasm, and Marshman found the sensation altogether pleasurable, and so he shook her again.

This time her spasm was more powerful, her legs shooting apart so that he penetrated deep inside her and set off another response, her interior muscles clutching at the head of his prick.

He shook her repeatedly by the throat, and her spasms became wilder and wilder. His erection grew and grew. He penetrated deeper and deeper, setting off more and more spasms, which excited him to jerk more and more frantically at her slender neck.

He didn't notice the blood that was pouring from her nose and mouth, any more than that which was pouring out of her vagina and drenching his loins. All he knew was that, at last, he was getting out of a woman something like what he had imagined sexual satisfaction to be.

In a final prolonged surge he ejaculated, his big arms pumping in time to his spurting semen, hammering the girl's head into the floor, his fat hands crushing her windpipe, breaking her neck.

He didn't hear the bones crack or feel her body go limp. He felt nothing but the enormous tide of his own orgasm, which went on and on until, at last, he collapsed, spent, into the mess of body and blood that lay beneath him.

"Well," he tittered in drunken exultation as he began to realize what had happened, "at least I've had a decent fuck at last, even if I did have to fuck the slut to death to do it." He giggled again and collapsed happily into sleep.

He stirred after a little time and was revolted to find himself covered in some stinking, sticky mess. He realized dimly that he was lying on something, and when the flickering light of the lamp revealed the still unconscious form of Jiyan's brother on the floor beside them, he began to recollect.

When full realization struck him, he leaped up, the sticky mess of Jiyan's blood making a sucking noise as the length of his body parted from hers.

"Good Lord, what a frightful mess. I've got to get out of here."

He found a small pail of water and upended it over his head, using the single blanket from the bed to wipe away most of the blood. Then he donned his uniform and ran out into the strangely deserted street. Not a ricksha in sight. He set off in a shambling run in the direction of the British army barracks.

"What a mess," he panted to himself as he ran. "What a shocking awful mess."

As soon as he reached the first turn in the narrow, twisting street, a dozen forms came out from the shadows and, one by one, entered the Feis' two-room shanty.

Hisses of astonishment gave way to wails of anguish, and then to roars of anger. More and more people came from neighboring shanties. All of them had heard the blows and cries, but none had wished to intervene, or even acknowledge their awareness to themselves. It was common knowledge that, where foreign devils were concerned, the only safe course was to stay as far away as possible.

But now the wails and angry shouts grew and grew, until, at last, the sleeping ward watchman was aroused and he came, belching and farting and scratching himself awake to see what had happened to disturb his sleep.

Fei Qili was revived, only to collapse again in grief and exhaustion from the severe beating he had endured. When he was again revived, he struggled to get back to unconsciousness rather than hear that his only sister had gone to join their long-dead parents and their other ancestors, and that now he must be the sole support of the family.

How could a boy support himself, let alone two children? A girl always had something to sell, and there were things for a boy to do around the girl. But what could a boy alone do?

None of the neighbors mentioned the British officer to the watchman. Nor did Qili. In the first place, it wasn't necessary; this was hardly a Chinese type of crime, and all the customers for the girls of the district came from the British barracks, or from British ships in the harbor. In the second place, only bad could come from foreign devils, even from talking about them. What difference did it make that one more Chinese had been killed by one more British soldier? A report to the British authorities would only bring much welcome attention to the neighborhood. Better to get on with the business of survival.

CHAPTER FOUR

Casca had deemed Lieutenant Marshman's execution perfectly just. His knowledge of the local language enabled him to hear the rumors from the Chinese barrack slaves. He had hurried to the red-light district early that afternoon, and had heard the whole story from Fei Jiyun's neighbors.

That same night he caught the subaltern returning late from yet another drunken carouse, and dragged him by the throat the width of the parade ground, one massive forearm choking off the officer's desperate attempts to shout for help, to the flagpole where he had strung him up.

Casca tautened the flag halyard until Marshman's feet just touched the ground, the noose in the rope not quite cutting off his breath.

The fat man struggled to support his weight on his toes while his fat fingers sought to prize the rope away from his neck. A very fit athlete might have had some chance, but Marshman's flabby musculature was not equal to the task. He could barely manage to breathe, and his attempts to shout for help produced nothing more than a hoarse wheeze.

Casca stepped back a pace and looked the purple-faced officer in the eye.

"Hanging is too good for you. You murdered a woman

I liked very much, and you have condemned her family to probable starvation. Now you're going to get some idea of what it's like to be fucked to death.''

He swung away, pivoting on his heel, to swing back again and sink his size-ten British army boot into Marshman's groin with all of his two hundred pounds of bone and muscle behind it, crushing the ruins of testicles and penis into the mess of shattered pelvic bone.

First Lieutenant Marshman tried to do several things at once, and failed at all of them.

He tried to bring up his knees to wrap his legs around his frightful injury; he tried to clutch at his balls with his hands; he tried to scream; he tried to breathe.

As his feet left the ground for an instant, the noose tightened around his throat. His hands, which had been sweeping downward for his balls, reached back up to try more desperately than before to claw the rope away from his neck. Although his nails tore his throat to bloody shreds, he failed to get a finger between rope and neck. No sound came from his mouth. No air entered his lungs.

As his weight sagged onto his feet, his legs pushed upward into the ruined mess of his pelvis, and again he tried to scream, tried to draw up his legs to curl his body into a fetal knot, tried with his hands to clutch at his groin.

Casca watched as the man dangling from the rope flapped his arms and legs like some fat bird in a trap.

Marshman's lungs were trying to expel their stale air. His lungs were also trying to drag in some fresh air. His heart was struggling to pump against the increasing pressure of the blocked lungs. His tongue was forced out through his teeth, where it swelled mightily until the agonized grinding of his teeth chewed it through. It dropped to the ground at his feet. Casca watched as the man's desperate flappings grew wilder and then suddenly stopped, the hands falling limply to his sides.

He saw the lieutenant's cap where it had fallen and kicked it away; then, struck by a thought, he picked it up and placed it on Marshman's head. He headed for his quarters, skirting the moonlit parade square as British soldiers are trained to do when not on parade.

During what was left of the night Marshman's weight stretched the rope and the length of his own body until his feet rested flat on the ground, his capped head held erect by the taut noose. Then rigor mortis began to set in.

At first light the Chinese barrrack slaves arrived to sweep clean the parade square, and the flies and the stench alerted them to the corpse.

Every Chinese for miles around knew of the murder in the shantytown and of the involvement of a British officer, and they were pleased to see one dead, no matter who or why.

It took a little longer for the troops, arriving for early-morning parade, to realize that the uniformed figure standing by the flag at attention was not quite what it appeared. The area close to the flagpole was officer territory, and the closest soldiers were too far away to discern the swollen features and the dried blood as they stood about knuckling sleep from their eyes, farting and scratching as they waited for parade to start.

A few noticed the strange rigidity of the office by the flagpole. Odd to have an officer there anyway. An interested murmur was still sweeping through the ranks when Regimental Sergeant Major Forster approached the flagpole, followed by two corporals with the flag, then a small knot of officers, and, finally, the colonel of the regiment.

The RSM pranced toward the flagpole as he had every morning for seventeen years. His black boots gleamed in the early-morning sun. His fresh-shaven face shone, as did every brass button on his red parade tunic and the brass nob on the blackwood stick tucked into his armpit. He was so absorbed in his own performance that the corpse by the flagpole moved him only to the thought: 'Ullo, what's a flippin' subaltern doin' on parade afore me?

And then: Stands more like a sarmajor than a hoffiser.

And then: Jesus Christ Almighty, he's fuckin' dead.

For the first time in thirty years' army service the career base wallah was confronted with an unexpected dead body.

Worse. He had to do something about it. And now.

He had one red-striped leg up in the air in the ridiculous "Sergeant Major on Parade" gait that was the pride of RSMs, and the despair of the rest of the army.

Everywhere around the parade ground there were men picking their noses, combing their hair, scratching their armpits.

"Well," he mumbled, "that's orright for 'em. They ain't on parade yet. And anyway, they're only flippin' ordinary soldiers. But Regimental Sergeant Major Forster is bloody well on parade, and that's that."

But, in spite of himself, his stride faltered, and he came to a quite unmilitary standstill, the two flag corporals coming to a confused halt just short of running into him.

"Lord almighty. This fucker really is dead," he bellowed.

The exclamation carried across a parade ground suddenly brought to brisk attention and alert silence by the unprecedented sight of an RSM coming off parade.

Even the officers awoke briefly from their hangovers, and one or two spoke. " 'Ullo, what's up?"

"Cripes, old Forster's lost his step."

Forster turned around—to see the sort of parade ground that was an RSM's dream. Not a head or a hand or a hair moved, not a tongue spoke. Nobody even seemed to breathe.

The officers (useless bloody lot, Forster thought) spoiled the show. They had been approaching the parade at a leisurely stroll as befits gentlemen who have breakfasted well and are looking forward to nothing more significant than a splendid lunch. But now they had broken into a nervous sort of shuffle, not at all army-style, rather like a bunch of anxious schoolboys.

"Bleedin' perishers," Forster fumed to himself. "But what the fuck am I to do?"

An idea came to him, the first in his life. He tried to put it from him.

"What? Give away a perfectly lovely parade like this? Not bleedin' likely," he hissed through clenched teeth.

But somehow his long-subdued intelligence convinced him that the officer by the flagpole was going to spoil the parade anyway. His routine-soaked mind yielded the point and he found himself shouting:

"Par-a-ade. Dis-miss!"

The startled soldiers sprang to attention. The officers stopped dead, blundering into each other.

"Rotten fuckers," Forster spit out. It was all going wrong. He had known it would. "That's what comes of ideas." Well, nothing for it now, but to go on with it. His well-trained base camp mind knew that there could be nothing more important than to ensure that the despised rank and file should know nothing of how or why an officer might have met with such a bizarre death.

"All noncommissioned men return to barracks im-me-di-ate-ly! Parade will come to attention at six-thirty ack emma." For good measure he added another "Dis-miss!"

This time even the officers got it right. They came off parade and hurried over to the flagpole as the troops obediently left the square in a buzz of confused conjecture. Colonel Braithwaite hurried his pace and the other officers slowed theirs so that he was able to take the lead as they all reached the corpse.

"Good Lord," the colonel breathed. "The new chappie, the drunk rotter. Anybody know this fellah's name?"

Captain Fotheringham sniffed disdainfully. "That mess is what used to be called Marshman."

"Yes. That's the name. Blighter can't hold his liquor. Not much loss. Going to look damned bad in dispatches though."

He turned to the RSM. "Well, cut him down, man. Cut him down."

Forster turned to pass the order on to the flag corporals, only to find that they had followed his order and left the parade ground.

"Rotten fuckers," Forster seethed. "Oh, won't I make it hard for them."

Each of the flag corporals wore a bayonet, as did every man on parade—except the RSM and the officers who carried only swagger sticks.

Colonel Braithwaite carried a crooked walking cane, a sign that he came from a Highland regiment. He saw the dilemma even as he realized that this impertinent RSM had, without so much as a nod from him, sent every bayonet back to the barracks.

Forster came smartly to attention. "Wish to report, sir. Don't have a knife, sir."

The colonel smiled to himself and muttered, "Insubordinate bastard." Aloud he said: "What's that, RSM? No knife?"

"No knife, sir."

"Well then, let's have one, Sarmajor."

"Yes sir. Will go off parade to get knife, sir."

He saluted, stood briefly at attention, then turned and marched RSM-style across the parade square in the direction of his office. As he stepped off the hallowed area of the parade square his stride changed to the rather more sane standard British army march step.

"When I get to my office, I'm going to give those two fucking corporals bloody hell."

The officers withdrew upwind of the corpse and took out cigarettes. But time passed and the RSM did not return.

Forster arrived at his office to find it locked and empty. The flag corporals had followed his orders to the letter and were now comfortably stretched out in their barracks telling and retelling all of the rumors that had swept the camp during the past twenty-four hours.

Regimental sergeants major did not demean themselves by carrying their keys, or anything else, on parade. Parade uniforms did not have even a single pocket. Forster's custom at the end of each morning's parade was to order the two flag corporals to check that all was well and tidy around the parade area while he strode off to his office. There he expected to find both of them waiting for him, one at attention inside, the other on guard outside.

But, even if he had his keys, he knew there was no spare bayonet anywhere in his office. Nor a knife of any sort. RSM Forster would have charged any man silly enough to bring to his office any item not on the list of prescribed equipment.

He looked around for a runner and realized that there was none. Not a man in sight. And the corporal's huts were on the other side of the barracks.

"Oh, Jesus, am I going to serve those two bastards some misery."

He set out in the direction of the corporals' quarters, but after he had marched a little he started to worry about the time that was passing. With a sudden awful thrill of panic he realized that he had set the new parade for six-thirty.

"What time is it now?" He stopped dead in consternation.

He had never been able to dream of affording a watch. On retirement, maybe an unmarried RSM might just afford one, but for him it was out of the question. The wife he never saw (her doctor said China was bad for her) soaked up every penny of his pay with her doctor's bills in

Brighton. It didn't seem to concern the doctor that Brighton was bad for her, too.

Forster's panic grew as he tried to think of where he could find a clock.

In his office. Certainly, but not where he could see it looking in from outside. That would make life too easy for the men in the ranks. Most orders around the base were set to the time of day, but no ordinary soldier had a watch, and the entire barracks was organized so that the few clocks boasted by Her Majesty's Forty-second Foot Regiment were almost always out of sight of the rank and file.

The clock in the RSM's office was on the wall opposite his desk where it could not be seen by any soldier facing him at attention. Nor could it be seen through the window by any trembling miscreant waiting outside. This included, at the moment, a very frustrated RSM Forster.

The officers' mess!

That wasn't too far away. But his steps slowed. He wasn't an officer. The clock was on the inside front wall of the entrance foyer, and it would be an unheard-of trespass for an NCO to step inside that foyer unsummoned.

And damned humiliating, too.

This imitation of a soldier lived for petty dominance. He put up with China and isolation and loneliness and near-celibacy for the thrills he enjoyed from exerting his rank and his almost unlimited disciplinary powers. He would suffer agonies of humiliation to trespass on upper-class territory where his rank was insignificant and even irrelevant.

The warrant officers' mess!

It wasn't all that much farther away, and not only was it his own mess, but he was the highest-ranking man in it. Actually he would have to pass both the officers' and the sergeants' messes. But to appear at the mess of his sergeant inferiors in the role of message boy was even more unthinkable than to enter the realm of the officer caste.

He hurried along, and was through the doors of the foyer and eyeing the clock before he had thought that there had been nobody to snap to attention for him.

Six-fifteen. Thank the lord. Plenty of time. But, where the hell was everybody?

He stomped through the building without encountering anybody until he came to the passage to the kitchens, where he was greeted by a grease bespattered cook's helper.

"Oh, ullo Sarmajor, wot brings you 'ere at this hour?"

Foster jerked to an infuriated halt.

"Attenshun?" he bellowed.

"Wot? Oh, blimey." Reluctantly Private Brian Warren came to attention.

"Why aren't you on parade?" Forster bellowed in an irrational outrage at the slovenly soldier.

"Wot sir? Cooks on parade?"

"Don't call me sir. I'm not a hoffiser."

A spark of rationality lit somewhere in what had once been the RSM's mind.

Cooks on parade? Of course cooks didn't go on parade. Thank God. They would make a decent parade impossible. The British army used for its ordinary cooks only those men who proved totally useless at everything else. Of course, they were useless as cooks, too, but somebody had to do it.

Forster turned away from the dirty cockney and marched into the stinking steam of the mess kitchen. He ignored the grimy morons sweating over their open caldrons and snatched a large butcher knife from a bench. He marched back toward the foyer and, at the doorway, almost ran into and very nearly disemboweled Private Warren, who was slouching his way through it.

The clock now said six-twenty, and Forster stepped out smartly, cursing himself that he had not had the sense to go to the kitchen door of the officers' mess for the knife, and to hell with the time and his dignity.

By the flagpole the officers were no happier than the RSM.

Parades were the very stuff of army life to sergeants major, but for officers they were nothing but a pain in the arse. All this time could have been much better spent at the billiard table, or reading the *Times*, or checking on the condition of the polo ponies.

The gruesomely rigid corpse of their brother officer was not smelling any better as the sun's heat increased, and the buzzing flies were paying almost as much attention to the live officers as to the dead one. The cigarettes helped a little, but not enough.

Colonel Braithwaite glowered as he looked over his officers for a victim. No help for it, they were more or less on parade, so any humiliation would have to be heaped upon the most junior officer. A pity, because Second Lieutenant Marksby was fast becoming something of a favorite with the colonel. But to choose anybody else would smack of favoritism. He could get away with that in the mess, but not on parade.

"Dammit Marksby," he snapped, "surely you have a knife, don't you?"

The faintly effeminate Marksby smiled in embarrassment.

"I, er, I do have a small pair of scissors, sir."

"Scissors?"

Blushing, the youth took from a pocket a small leather manicure pouch. He took from it a pair of nail scissors and tentatively proffered them.

The colonel stepped back and waved a hand at the corpse. "Well, cut the damned thing down, won't you?"

Marksby approached the grisly remains of his fellow subaltern and promptly threw up. The sky reeled, the ground came up to meet him, and Second Lieutenant

Marksby lost his interest in First Lieutenant Marshman, the British army, and all else as he pitched unconscious to the ground.

"Barrett," the colonel barked at another subaltern. "Get that scissors and get this thing down off that rope."

"Yes sir." The young man moved quickly to snatch up the scissors and went to work with it on the rope.

The soldiers returning for parade arrived to see Second Lieutenant Boy Barrett, one of the few officers they respected, scraping the nail scissors through the flag halyard one thread at a time.

From the far end of the parade ground Regimental Sergeant Major Forster approached in his high-stepping formal gait, stick under one arm, the huge butcher knife in the other swinging fist. He ignored the shorter diagonal and marched carefully the full length of the parade ground before stamping his way through a ceremonial left turn to march toward the flagpole.

As the corpse crashed to the ground beside the fainted lieutenant, he stirred and got to his feet.

This appalling display of shoddy parade ground behavior almost brought the RSM to a halt halfway to the flagpole. Well, he thought, it can't get any worse.

From somewhere in the assorted uniformed ranks there came a giggle. Then, from another quarter a chuckle, then several, and then great guffaws of laughter came from all over the parade ground.

Sergeant Cass Longman was laughing as lustily as any of his soldiers at the comic entertainment being provided by the officers of the regiment. He felt much closer to his men than he did to the officer caste, or to the strutting absurdity of an RSM. The other sergeants felt the same way. The officers were making fools of themselves; so what? It was always open season on officers if you didn't happen to be one.

Barrett stooped to lift the corpse by the shoulders. Marksby, slightly recovered, stooped to help. Their heads crashed and they fell apart to either side of the corpse.

The ranks whooped delightedly. Gales of laughter rocked back and forth across the parade ground as the two dazed subalterns staggered back to their feet to stoop again, managing this time to avoid each other, but between them only succeeding in jerking the corpse to a sitting position.

Two more second lieutenants sprang forward and took the heels.

"What a fuck-up," Colonel Braithwaite fumed. "Well, at least we're out of it now."

He was about to snap the order to take the corpse away when the panting RSM arrived and came noisily to attention before him.

The laughter stopped. Forster forced his aching lungs to bellow at their best parade ground blast.

"Wish to report sir, I've brought the knife."

"An' just in time, too, mate," a wag hollered from the ranks, and the parade ground exploded in a new burst of hilarity. Cheers, jeers, hoots, catcalls, and whistles came from everywhere.

The troops had now reached a situation they relished. Strictly speaking, it was difficult to make laughing an offense. Like sneezing or farting, it often had to be tolerated. Besides, the soldiers had not yet been called on parade. Best of all, any disciplinary action would have to be applied to the entire regiment. And any such punishment would have to be reported in dispatches, and the soldiers knew that this was a situation that the colonel would not want to report.

The troopers in the ranks had learned what they knew of their duties and privileges and how the army worked through the toughest possible school, and the little they did know they knew very damned well.

Similar thoughts were running through the colonel's mind. Damn this fool RSM. He should have scrubbed the parade altogether. What the devil to do now?

Well, the main thing was to ensure that the ranks knew as little as possible of this officer's demise. He opened his mouth again to order the removal of the body, when RSM Forster's routine-steeped, discipline-dominated mentality snatched the moment from him.

"On the order, parade will come to attention," Forster bellowed. "Pa-rade, at-ten-shun."

But there came no answering stomp of heels on the ground. Instead the volume of mirth increased as if his command had been intended as an addition to the entertainment.

The colonel found his voice at last. "Get this sack of lard out of here," he snapped to the officers holding Marshman's body. "Take it to sick bay—and not a word to anybody."

Boy Barrett turned disgustedly to carry the corpse away.

"Past every bloody private soldier in the regiment, like the trash detail," he cursed under his breath at the absurdity of trying to keep the matter quiet. But he squared his shoulders and stepped out as if honored to be carrying a fellow officer who had died in the line of duty.

The other three junior officers followed his lead, and it was almost enough.

But the colonel was now determined to revenge himself upon the RSM for preempting his authority.

"RSM," he barked, "get this parade to order."

Forster stamped his way through the ridiculous routine it took to bring a regimental sergeant major to attention. Then he saluted, stamped his way through an about turn, and faced the troops.

Coming right after his hilariously mistimed arrival with the knife, this performance had the effect of continuing the comedy act, the huge butcher knife alongside the swagger stick under his left arm.

The troops applauded lustily, some of them wondering how they had so long watched this ritual of one man ceremonially parading himself without laughing before.

All the officers withdrew while Forster repeatedly made a fool of himself, shouting at the now quite uncontrollable troops.

Sergeant Longman grew bored with the entertainment and decided to take a hand. He had better things to do than watch a fool on ceremonial display.

He spoke quietly to his own corporals.

"Murphy, O'Hara, Smith, quiet down, will you? Get ready to go off parade."

The three corporals stopped chuckling and turned to their men with serious faces. Taking their cue from Casca, they spoke quietly but forcefully.

"Orright then you lot. Orright then. Enuff's enuff. It ain't May Day you know. Quiet down will youse."

Casca's men suddenly found themselves outside the comfortable anonymity they had been enjoying. One by one each soldier mastered his merriment as he faced his own corporal and, beyond him, Sergeant Longman, who stood as if waiting expectantly and a little impatiently.

In a few moments Casca's men were all silent.

"On the order dismiss, move to the right and dismiss to await further orders," Casca rushed out in one breath, then: "Dis-miss!"

His troops made the required turn, then walked from the parade ground.

The surprised sergeant of the next platoon looked at Casca, who shrugged as if to say: "It's easy enough when you know how." The sergeant promptly started to bring his own men under control.

The roars of laughter died down to a hubbub of chuckles

and then to silence as one company after another was brought under control.

Forster was the last to realize that the circus was over and was still bellowing uselessly for the parade to come to order as the last few squads were leaving the field.

Colonel Braithwaite decided to be magnanimous and came to his rescue. He moved a little closer.

"Very good, sarmajor. New parade in five minutes, thank you."

"New parade five minutes sir." Forster went through his lonely routine stamping through his turn as he dismissed himself to march in solitary absurdity to the edge of the parade ground, where he could wait out the five minutes.

The troops were well content to have gotten away with so much, and they settled down to wait, which was, after all, their main day-to-day activity.

CHAPTER FIVE

Casca had not given much thought to the consequences when he had carried about the execution, and had certainly not expected to be apprehended.

But he had reckoned without the inexplicable workings of a Chinese mind.

The dead whore's younger brother had spent the previous night seeking out Lieutenant Marshman in his next debauch, and in the early hours of the morning, had followed the lieutenant to the army camp, intent upon himself taking revenge for his sister's murder. But he had been unable to sneak past the guard at the barracks gate for some little time, and when he again caught up with the staggering lieutenant, it was just in time to see Casca seize him and drag him to the flagpole.

He had been afraid to go any closer, but he witnessed the hanging, and knew that the hangman had been a sergeant.

When the news swept the marketplace the next morning, Fei Qili had gone to the barracks, and had reported what he knew, confident that the result would be the death of yet another of the hated white devils.

To the little Chinese boy, all foreign devils looked much alike; they were all enormous, with strangely colored eyes and hair. His description would have been too vague to be of any use, but Colonel Braithwaite had called Sergeant Cass Longman to assist the Chinese interpreter.

As Casca stepped into the colonel's office the startled Fei Qili recognized him as the hangman, and blurted out: "This is the man."

The Chinese interpreter immediately translated, and the colonel exploded: "So you're the mystery sergeant. What the fuck do you think you're doing, hanging my lieutenants?"

Fei Qili had now also recognized this big sergeant as a friend of his sister who had been kind to the family. He stared at Casca in consternation as he realized that he was betraying his sister's avenger. Well, so the fates had decided.

Casca saw that there was no way out for him. There were not that many sergeants on the base, and few who could have singlehandedly dealt with the large officer. And no others with a motive. Indeed, there was not another man in the barracks who could be moved to give a damn about the murder of a Chinese harlot.

"Dammit," the colonel snapped, "there's no bloody shortage of whores, and we're damned short of officers— even if he was a no-good, drunken, murderous slob. And now I suppose I'll have to hang you as well, and we're damned short of sergeants, too."

He had Casca thrown into a cell to await trial, and had gone to the Army and Navy Club to drink away the nuisance of it all.

The colonel was pleased to see that the club was already quite busy as colonial service army, and China Company officers took their first gin and quinine for the day, the essential preventive medicine in the pestilential tropics.

He took a leather chair at the British consul's table and motioned to the Chinese servant standing by the oak-paneled wall. He brought to the table a tray carrying a carafe, linen napkins, a gasogene, an ice bucket, and quinine.

"Another Taiping Rebellion is what we're facing," the pink-faced consul mumbled into his pink gin. "Fanatical bloody heathens shouting mixed-up garbage compounded out of the bloody Bible and that fool Marx's socialist crap."

"Ridiculous nonsense, of course," the colonel replied, shaking out his month-old copy of the London *Daily Mail*. "Never should have taught the blighters to read. Bad business all round. Bound to cause trouble."

"Teach the Chinese to read?" The consul looked up from his drink. "They were reading and writing thousands of years ago."

"There you are then," said the colonel. "We should have known better than to let them see books in English. These bloody missionaries are to blame."

"Well, whoever's to blame, it looks like we're in for big trouble. And we can't even find out what's happening in the countryside until it blows up in our faces, like it did last time. And last time, you recall, they gave us no bloody end of strife. Took us fourteen bloody years to pacify the country, and—"

"I say," the colonel interrupted him, "listen to the *mail* about the Chinese: 'It is because there are people like this in the world that there is an Imperial Britain. This sort of creature had to be ruled, so we rule him, for his good and our own.' Damned right.

"Send out a scout." The colonel dismissed the problem as he waved at the Chinese servant for another drink.

"A scout?" The consul was incredulous. "How many men do you have who can speak Chinese?"

"Only one I know of, and now I've got to hang him," the colonel replied unhappily.

The consul's head snapped up from his drink. "You do have a man who speaks Chinese?"

"Did have. Damn fool killed that new subaltern, the drunk oaf—Marshman, I think his name was. Marshman choked his whore."

"The flagpole executioner?" asked the consul.

"That's him. He'll be at the end of a rope in a day or two himself."

"You could pardon him if he volunteered for a suicide mission."

"Sure I could. You got one?"

"Yes, I think I may have. Look, I'm going to go and see the ambassador. Be a good chap and don't hang this blighter for a bit. Hanging our own always looks bad to the Chinks anyway."

The colonel shrugged as the consul hurried away, and the next day Casca was again paraded before the colonel.

Casca had quite resigned himself to hanging, although death now held more terror for him than it ever had.

During his time in the cell, his sleep, and even his waking moments, had been disturbed by recollections of that day on Golgotha when the Jew preacher had cursed him as he withdrew the spear from his side.

"Soldier, you are content with what you are. So that you shall remain until we meet again."

Then he relived the moment when he had brushed the sweat from his face with the back of his hand, and the blood that had run down the spear shaft touched his tongue, to send him crashing to the ground in a poisoned stupor.

In the succeeding nineteen hundred years Casca had died countless deaths, and with each one his death agony, whatever it had been, had been resuffered as his body painfully put itself back together to fulfill the Nazarene's curse. Even more than the unbearable death agony, he dreaded the inevitable reawakening to the increasingly horrible realization that he was alive once again, to do nothing other than fight for pay, until he was killed once more, and the cycle began all over again.

And this time, he was doing it because of a whore, just as he had so many times before—although not all of the women he had died for had had the decency to admit their calling, even to themselves.

"Well, all right then, nothing to do but face it."

He smiled at the thought that once hanged he'd be out of the British army. What had pressed him to join in the first place?

"Nothing to laugh about what?" the colonel's bark interrupted his reverie. "You're going to hang, you know."

Casca looked calmly at this second-rate colonial time server, a barely passable soldier by any standard.

" 'Spose we all deserve hanging one way or the other—sir."

Colonel Braithwaite could scarcely believe his ears. Had this swine really said "we," meaning that there was some sort of commonality between a mere bloody sergeant and an officer and gentleman who carried Her Majesty's commision?

"Jesus," he swore under his breath, "the consul can go to hell. I'm going to hang this blighter for his fucking impertinence."

Casca caught a glimpse of Braithwaite's mind and realized that he had not been brought into the colonel's exalted presence merely to be told his fate. Something else was afoot. And if there was an alternative to dancing at the end of a rope, Casca was all for it—whatever it might be.

"We of we in the ranks, that is, sir," he added in meek, lower-caste submission, bobbing his head obsequiously, as British army sergeants were somehow trained to do, allowing the infuriated colonel room to reinflate himself above common soldier level.

The caste cringe was no more a problem for Casca than one more trick in sword play. Early in his British army career, he had discerned that those who couldn't do it never made it past corporal, and his mouth had hung agape at the resultant waste of some of the very best material.

But, fuck it, it was the price of joining the game, and, at the time, Casca had been right out of a game. So he had joined the branch of the British China Company known as the British army, and accepted the archaic class divisions just as he accepted the inedible food and the intolerable discipline.

Well, the somewhat mollified colonel thought, let it go for now. This Johnny will give me another chance to hang him sooner or later. Aloud he said: "I have considered this unfortunate matter carefully from all angles, and I believe it may be within my power to offer you a way to save your worthless life."

Casca saw clearly that, for some reason, the colonel had little choice but to offer him his life, but prudence suggested a humble approach.

"And what way might that be, sir?" he asked as ingratiatingly as he could manage.

"Can't imagine why you ever bothered, but you speak the abominable system of grunts and gasps these yellow beasts call a language, don't you?"

"I speak some Chinese, yes. As for why I learned it, I might recommend it to you, sir, as an intellectual exercise."

"Wha-a-at? So I can talk to my laundress or the ricksha boys, or the whores? What the fuck do you think I should want to say to them in their own tongue?"

"There are other Chinese, sir, and it might help you to appreciate their mentality."

"If there were one to appreciate in the species." The colonel didn't intend to pursue this discussion. "Report to the regimental sergeant major. He will arrange conduct to the consul, who will outline a mission to you. If you accomplish it successfully, I just might be dissuaded from hanging you on your return. Dismiss."

As Casca saluted, the colonel added: "You're still under arrest, mind."

"Yes, sir," Casca answered easily. "I shall ask the consul for formal release from arrest—if I agree to the mission."

He turned in fine British army style and marched from the room, feeling on top of the world.

Harry Hargreaves, the British consul, was one of the best of the colonial service men in Hong Kong. He had once had hopes of an appointment in the Indian civil service, but his qualifications—"character," "all rounder," "steel true and blade straight"—determined that he went to the colonial service side of the Foreign Office quadrangle at the corner of Whitehall and Downing Street in London.

On the other side of the quadrangle Indian civil service cadets were being examined in horsemanship and English literature, the prescribed qualifications.

He had accepted the Hong Kong post, which nobody in the diplomatic corps wanted, for the sake of his career. He had been born well rather than rich, and that made him ideal diplomatic material; but it also meant that he could not afford to idle his time away in Paris or Budapest or St. Petersburg. He needed postings where there was work to be done, where he could get some chance to exhibit his talents and his capacity for work.

So far Hong Kong had not provided either, but it was his personal conviction that trouble was brewing, and if he could be instrumental in nipping it in the bud, it could help his career enormously.

He looked at the heavily built sergeant who stood at attention on the other side of his walnut desk. His glance fell to Casca's gleaming boots.

Captain Graeme Maclaine, the poor, young Scots doctor who had come to China in the hope of saving enough of his army pay to one day buy a small highland medical practice, had certified the cause of Marshman's death as being heart failure, brought about by suffocation, induced in turn by strangulation. He had also noted massive internal injuries and hemorrhage as the result of damage inflicted upon the genital and pelvic areas with a blunt instrument wielded with considerable force. The postmortem report ended with a note that the corpse lacked a tongue, which appeared to have been bitten off.

The consul had no way of knowing that one of the Chinese slaves who swept the parade ground had found the tongue, and that it was now drying in the sun like a piece of beef jerky, on the back sill of Fei Qili's shanty.

The consul brought his eyes back to Casca's face.

"Do you have anything to say for yourself?"

"In what connection, sir?"

Cool customer, the consul thought. Too damned cool. "In connection," he said aloud, "with the murder of First Lieutenant Marshman."

"I deny any connection with the execution for murder of the lieutenant."

"What the hell are you talking about? There is no question of execution. Marshman was not accused of any murder. You are here charged with his murder."

"And I deny it," Casca lied blandly. "But, it seems to me that whoever did the rotter in did the army a service."

"Enough!" the consul shouted. "Sergeant Longsman, you forget yourself."

"Just a simple soldier, sir." Casca tugged ironically at

his forelock. "But I do hear that the Chinese are rather pleased about it, and, at first news of the girl's murder, there was talk of rebellion in the bazaars."

The consul glared at Casca in exasperation. Dammit, the fellow was right. The drunken lecher could have set off just the sort of explosion he was worried about.

·Well all right, maybe this chappie was entitled to some sort of fit reward for possibly saving China for the empire. A medal would hardly do. Perhaps a small exgratia payment to his widow, for he most certainly should be hanged anyway. Can't have bloody sergeants killing officers.

"Sergeant Longman, I understand that you speak Chinese, and the ambassador and the colonel have empowered me to temporarily release you from arrest, should you agree to put that capacity to work on behalf of the empire."

"I'll be glad to do what I can for the empire, sir."

"Mmmm. You mentioned rebellion. Do you know any facts about such a thing? Ringleaders, meeting, stuff like that?"

"No sir, of course not."

"No? No, I suppose not. Well, we're pretty sure there's trouble brewing, and we want to know more. In brief, we want you to go out into the countryside as a political intelligence scout, undercover of course, and see what you can find out."

"I suppose I could do that, sir." Not too bad, Casca thought. Maybe they'll pass me off as a businessman, or a missionary. "What sort of cover do you have in mind?"

"Cover? No idea. That's up to you. Just keep out of sight and keep a good lookout and keep us informed up to the minute. That's all."

Casca looked down at his own bulk. "Stay out of sight, sir?"

"Well, dress like a Chinese. Surely you can manage something."

"There ain't many Chinese my size, sir. And there ain't none with blue eyes or fair hair."

"Then keep your damned eyes and hair out of sight."

The consul was exasperated again. This lower-class cad was behaving exactly as one would expect a lower-class cad to behave—looking for some easy way to do the job, instead of just getting on with it. Terrible, the low-grade material we have to work with out here.

"One of those big cane hats should hide your hair and your eyes, shouldn't it?"

"Well, perhaps," Casca parried, "we can just put off this assignment until I grow me a pigtail?"

The consul's head snapped up. No, the swine wasn't laughing. Well, enough of this.

"Sergeant Longman," he drawled, "we can put off the assignment forever if we choose to. But the bloody Chinks are not likely to put off their beastly uprising. And Braithwaite doesn't want to put off your hanging."

So, a few days later, Casca found himself on the steamer out of Hong Kong harbor.

His satchel carried a small fortune in gold and gems, some local currency, some English pounds, and a sizable cake of opium.

The consul's instructions were for Casca to make his way around the borders of Kwangtung Province to the neighboring provinces of Fukien, Kiangsi, Hunan, and Kwangsi, to see if he could discern signs of trouble brewing for the British regime.

"Put in some time on the rivers too," the consul had added offhandedly. "The Han and the Mei and the Tung and the Si. We'd like to know more about the traffic on them. And keep those reports flowing in. I want a message from you every time you get near contact with our communication network.

"Oh, and do keep an account of how you spend the funds. Must keep the books straight, you know. You might yet escape hanging for killing one of Her Majesty's subalterns, but, should you abscond with her funds, I assure you nothing shall save you. There will be no mercy.

"And don't think of deserting. There's nowhere for you to go where we can't find you. Be assured we will catch you sooner or later, and when we do, you will surely hang."

CHAPTER SIX

Casca was pulled from his reverie by the return of Ju Liqun, Songzhen's worthless husband, to their store. The little man arrived in the wake of his scurrying offspring, rolling along with the aimless gait of the perpetual drunkard. His bow was deep and ingratiating, but Casca noticed that his eyes were searching the corners of the small room as if in search of some of the promised money that the children had undoubtedly reported to him.

"Welcome, honorable barbarian, to my less-than-worthy abode and far-from-profitable business."

Casca bowed in reply. "Thank you, gracious host. I shall try to make myself worthy of your generous hospitality and your wife's excellent cooking, which I have already sampled with much pleasure."

"Ah, honorable one, you do us great honor. Please to make yourself at ease and to amuse yourself within these unworthy walls as if they are your own."

Casca bowed again and, thoroughly bored with the potentially endless exchange of courteous flatteries, he produced a handful of Chinese coins and paper money.

Ju Liqun's greedy little eyes lit up, then widened in unbelieving delight as Casca added one English pound to the pile.

Casca flicked his eyes over the far-from-inscrutable Chinese faces that were staring, goggle-eyed with greed, at the money in his hand.

"Oh fuck," he muttered to himself. "I've screwed up again."

His mind raced as he sought a way to undo the damage done by producing such an extravagant display of his enormous wealth. Even in Hong Kong an English pound note represented great riches. Here in this remote village it seemed like more money than even a rich man might dream of.

He handed the Chinese money to Liqun.

"Honorable host, please be so kind as to accept this payment in the valuable currency of your esteemed nation for the time of my stay in your respected residence.

"I also add this pound in English currency as an earnest of the urgency and delicacy of my mission. This pound also shall be yours when that mission is completed successfully."

It didn't work. All five Chinese heads swiveled toward Casca's pack where even greater wealth was obviously stored.

"Well," he said to himself, "so much for the carrot. Back to the stick."

He locked eyes with Ju Liqun and steeled his voice.

"This enormous reward"—and he plucked the pound from Liqun's hand—"is payment for the silence of you and your family, for which I am most happy to pay, rather than have to threaten you with the agonizing deaths that will result for all of you if you so much as breathe one word of my presence here."

He allowed the pound to fall back into Liqun's palm, and in turn fixed his eyes on each of the family's faces.

"Should my presence here become known outside of these walls, all of you will die, and die slowly and horribly. If anything should happen to my person, he who comes after me will ensure that even the most hideous death that you can dream of will be a pleasant and most merciful release compared to the endless tortures that he will devise.''

Ju Liqun fell to his knees. The old man and his daughter threw themselves on their faces at Casca's feet, and the two children groveled on the floor behind them.

"Oh, merciful, just, and most esteemed barbarian, please spare this humble family from your wrath," Ju Liqun whined, placing the money on the floor before Casca. "To serve your eminent excellence in your mission is for us an inestimable honor, and we need no recompense. I beg you, take back this money and allow us to serve you. Your blessed presence in our unworthy abode will be for us the most excellent and desirable reward." Ju Liqun prostrated himself.

Casca pondered a moment and, as nothing else came to mind, he placed his foot on Liqun's head. Well, he thought, at least they're suitably terrified, and I really have no alternative but to trust them—so long as I can see them.

He allowed some of his weight to rest on Liqun's head, then removed his foot and stepped back to stand, arms folded, a severe frown on his face.

Tremulously Ju Liqun looked up at him. Casca decided that he could afford to be gracious.

"Get up," he said, carefully omitting any courtesies. "Take the money. When my mission is completed another like me will come riding on a high horse, and he will reward you with yet another English pound."

Not bad, he said to himself. He was well pleased with this invention. Then he looked around and noticed that the rest of the family was still hunched over on the floor. He barked, "On your feet!"

Deng Ziyang got to his feet with considerable dignity.

"Honorable Cas-Ca Sho, if, in our unworthiness, we have displeased you, we apologize. You need have no fears of the reliability and discretion of this humble family. My unworthy son-in-law and my humble daughter and her insignificant children may be relied upon to serve you just as I have done in bringing you from Tsungkow." He bowed deeply, and the rest of the family got to their feet and bowed, too.

Casca felt compelled to admire the way the old man had claimed his due credit for doing a good job in hauling Casca, for an extravagant fee, to his daughter's house where his family could not expect to profit further from him.

Practical man, Casca mused.

He nodded his acceptance of these promises and reached for his sack. He took from it his clothes and some papers and books and a small rosewood box secured with a brass lock.

He handed the clothes to Songzhen. "Please wash these for me."

He gave the books and papers to Liqun. "These are the materials of my mission, and I entrust them to you. Kindly keep them for me in a secure place."

Casca suppressed a grin as he saw Liqun's eyes light up on the locked box, which, it so happened, contained nothing but writing materials.

He handed the box to Liqun. "And this, you must guard with your life."

Ju Liqun reached hungrily for the box, but as his hands closed on it Casca tightened his grip. His steely, blue-gray eyes glared into Liqun's black ones. "Should anything—*anything*—happen to this box, I assure you, you will live just long enough to wish that you had never been born."

The worst of Casca's fears were confirmed when he saw that Ju Liqun lusted so intensely to possess the box that his fingers did not slacken their grip, although his mouth dropped open and his eyes widened in fear.

"Honorable Cas-Ca Sho, please do not imagine that I will allow any harm to come to this treasure. I shall guard it as I do my own children."

Casca concealed his contempt for the drunk, as he glanced briefly at the ragged, unkempt boy and girl.

"And this," he said as he produced a much larger, elaborately carved camphor-wood chest, "is even more important. Do you dare to undertake its custody? You shall be rewarded well if it remains safe, or punished most atrociously should it come to harm."

This time Casca failed to suppress his grin as Liqun grabbed for the chest. But his smile went unnoticed as ten greedy eyes focused on the box full of expensive silks and satins.

"Your trust in me will serve you well, I assure you, most honorable Cas-Ca Sho."

Casca reached again into the sack and brought out the leather pouch in which he carried his toothbrush and shaving gear. He lifted the right side of his shirt to tuck this pouch into his belt, noticing again the hungry gleam in Liqun's eyes.

For a moment he toyed with the idea of allowing Ju Liqun to see the Webley in the left side of his belt, but decided to keep both the gun and the short knife sheathed behind his back for another occasion.

He kicked the sack casually into the corner, and was relieved to see that Liqun's eyes didn't follow it. For the moment his hoard of gold, gems, and drugs was unrevealed, if not quite safe. The promise of further reward, his dire threats, and the prospect of getting to the contents of the boxes and the leather pouch should keep Liqun and his family from betraying him for a while.

"The hell with it anyway, I need some rest," he muttered to himself, and asked Liqun where he might sleep.

Songzhen bowed deeply. "Honorable sir, please to just wait for one minute while I make ready our poor bedchamber for your exalted presence."

She left the room and Casca seated himself on the one small chair, stretching his legs so that his crossed heels happened to rest on the discarded sack. He closed his eyes and, ignoring the others in the room, commenced breathing deeply, willing his overtautened muscles to relax.

CHAPTER SEVEN

Casca dozed in the corner of Ju Liqun's store, but his heels didn't move off his satchel, and from time to time he opened one eye to glance around the small room and to listen to the sounds from the next room and from the street. Then he would drop back into a half sleep.

At least he was still alive, although the mission given him so casually by the consul appeared more and more suicidal by the moment.

Under the numerous treaties exacted from China by the colonial powers, any Christian's life was sacred, his safety a charge on the emperor, as stipulated by the 1858 Treaty of Tientsin: "The Christian religion inculcates the practice of virtue and teaches man to do as he would be done by." The treaty had brought to an end the British and French siege and eventual sacking of the city over the death of a French missionary who had been killed by bandits hundreds of miles away in the interior.

But for Casca to travel about in the style that might invoke the protection of the treaty would make his assignment impossible. The consul was well aware that his already existing intelligence-gathering network of missionaries, soldiers, and traders was not ever going to detect the type of signs that he wanted Casca to look for.

51

As an undercover spy, Casca was quite outside the protection of the treaties. If captured he would certainly be executed after being suitably tortured for information. Any Chinese who assisted him in any way risked the same treatment.

As Casca dozed he confirmed in his mind the plan that he was already working toward. He could not hope to remain undiscovered in any one place for more than a few days. Just his physical bulk astounded even the largest Chinese and aroused widespread comment amongst people who generally only came up to his elbow and were so lightly built that he could carry one under each arm and another one, or even two, on his back.

And just the color of his eyes was sufficient to betray him. Not only were there no blue-eyed Chinese, they did not even know of blue eyes, so that he was an object of wonder anywhere he was seen. And the wonder led to comment, discussion, and even alarm.

If he were to survive he had to carry out the assignment very quickly and make his way back to Hong Kong as fast as possible.

Casca had not been slow to provide the sort of evidence that the consul was looking for. He reasoned that the assignment would not be considered complete until the consul had in hand all the information he was seeking.

In each port and town that Casca had traveled through he had sought out the contact for the British intelligence network and sent a dispatch to the consul. He reported widespread resentment toward foreign devils, and especially the British. He exaggerated every instance of obstruction or lack of cooperation that he observed, and reported casual anti-British remarks as the rantings of agitators. He also reported widespread dissatisfaction with financial conditions, and assessed the general state of the society as unstable.

He had come to Shou-Chang in the hope of uncovering evidence of impending conflict. He had already decided that if the evidence happened to be insufficient, he would see to it that more evidence came to light, even if he himself had to foment a rebellion.

As it happened he need not have worried. Discontent was, indeed, everywhere and growing daily. China was a powder keg waiting only for a detonating spark.

When Ju Songzhen woke him to say that her own bedchamber was ready for its guest, Casca got up from the chair, put two fingers into his satchel strap, and casually lifted it just clear of the floor. He allowed it to swing there like a pendulum, and as he came to the doorway of the bedchamber he let it swing forward and released it so that it skated across the floor to come to rest in a corner.

The carefully wrapped gold and gems made no sound, and Casca thought he had adequately disguised the sack's real weight.

He turned in the doorway, effectively occupying the space beyond as his own private territory.

"Thank you my kind hosts. I am sure this chamber will be very satisfactory. Now I intend to rest."

He let the sack curtain fall in their faces.

He was moving to retrieve his satchel when an embarrassed cough came from the curtain, and he turned to see Liqun's face nervously peeping into the room.

"What is it?" Casca asked.

"Honorable barbarian Cas-Ca Sho," Ju Liqun said, coming into the room, "does not my humble wife Songzhen please you?"

"I find your wife and your house very pleasant and suited to my purpose, thank you."

Ju Liqun looked confused and worried. After a moment he plucked up the courage to speak again.

"Honorable Cas-Ca Sho, we are of the Hakka people, a

people who travel much. We understand the needs of travelers, and it affords us the highest gratification to provide for the pleasant relaxation of strangers who have been wearied by long journeys. The hospitable reception of strangers is agreeable to our deities, and draws down the blessing of increase upon our families, and ensures augment to our wealth and safety from dangers."

He waited expectantly, but Casca didn't speak for want of understanding where this conversation was headed.

"We are a poor and humble family, and my wife is an insignificant woman, but I humbly beg that you will take her for your pleasure."

He drew aside the sack curtain and gestured to where his wife stood in the doorway.

Her work clothes had been replaced by a close-fitting cheongsam that ended at her knees. Deep slits in the sides of the dress revealed shapely legs. Songzhen's almond eyes fluttered as she looked apprehensively at Casca, and he realized that she dreaded the possibility that he might reject her and so deprive her family of the much-needed goodwill of the gods.

Well, Casca thought, one shouldn't be ungracious, and I would not wish to cause embarrassment. He smiled and held out his hand to Songzhen and bowed to Liqun. "Thank you, generous host, for your kind hospitality. The gods will bless you for it."

Ju smiled and bowed, then withdrew to the other room. There was a great deal of noise, as if something heavy were being dragged about, and Ju Liqun reappeared in the doorway, dragging an iron tub full of steaming water. The two children were helping him, pushing the tub from behind. They smiled and left the room.

Songzhen indicated to Casca that he should undress and get into the tub, and he very readily did so.

Songzhen squatted beside him and soaped and washed his body thoroughly.

"Where does this hot water come from?" Casca asked in some wonder.

"Why, the water comes from the village pump, and it is heated in our yard. Like everybody else we love to bathe each day in hot water."

"But is it not expensive to heat the water?"

Songzhen laughed lightly. "Not at all, honorable guest, we have much coal in our yard."

"But where do you buy this coal?"

"But we do not buy it. It is always there. We dig for it."

Then Casca recalled that coal was, indeed, everywhere in this country and, in the main, only a few feet beneath the surface. Even the poorest people, he now remembered, were accustomed to bathing at least every few days. Those who were too poor to have their own tub went to public bathhouses where the water was heated at the expense of the community for the convenience of all.

He got out of the tub and Songzhen dried him carefully, then motioned for him to lie on the low, wide bed. She squatted beside him and anointed him all over with some sweetly scented oils, and then gently and thoroughly massaged his aching muscles.

By the time she was through Casca felt pleasantly relaxed and at ease.

Songzhen stood up and unlatched the cheongsam at the neck, allowing the garment to fall to reveal her small-breasted, slim-hipped but shapely body.

Not bad, Casca was thinking when she threw herself at him, grabbing him by the shoulders and biting him tenderly but hungrily on the neck while she rubbed the length of her body against his. Her little hands fluttered about like butterflies, now playing with his hair, now stroking his chest or fondling his testicles. All the while Songzhen continued to nibble at his body wherever her mouth happened to contact it.

Then she was astride him and he was inside her, her agile body pushing at him with a fierce energy that said clearly that it had been a long time since her drunken husband had satisfied her longings.

Casca readily devoted himself to the task, and in a little while Songzhen slept serenely beside him, a small smile of contentment on her face.

From the next room came the sound of the sleeping Liqun's heavy breathing. Worn out, Casca surmised, with his fruitless study of how to secretly open his two boxes.

So far so good. By tomorrow he will have given up on the boxes as impossible to open without obvious damage. He might then start thinking about Casca's other possessions, such as the leather pouch, full of diamonds perhaps, but in fact, of shaving gear. So he would continue to carry the pouch on his person and allow Liqun to see it from time to time, while using it to carry a portion of his valuables.

Which would leave only his satchel. Time to do something about that.

He crept out of the bed and explored the floor on his hands and knees, seeking a loose floorboard.

But, when he found one, the empty hollow beneath convinced him that he had found one of the Ju family hoards, no doubt just recently emptied while Songzhen had prepared the room for him.

He continued his search by the faint moonlight, and at last found what he was looking for—a gap between the wall and the first floorboard. He dug into the ground under the board, and soon produced a cache large enough for his valuables.

He put the opium, most of the English money, some

gold, and some diamonds in the small pouch, and buried the rest.

He carefully scraped all of the earth back into the gap, compacting the loose soil over his hoard so that even exploring fingers would find nothing but dirt. Then he took off his jacket and trailed it back and forth and around in circles until all traces of fresh dirt had been distributed all about the room.

He guessed that any time now Ju Liqun would awake and start thinking about his satchel, so he put his shaving gear in it and placed it where it could just be seen around the sack curtain. He had Liqun thinking it held nothing of value, so now he could find it so.

All the while he had kept one eye on Songzhen, but her eyelids had not so much as fluttered, nor had the smile left her lips.

For his amusement, he noted his satchel's position. He knew that when he awakened he would no doubt find it slightly moved. Thus noting its place in the room, he fell into an untroubled sleep.

CHAPTER EIGHT

As it happened, when he awoke the position of his sack was not one of Casca's immediate concerns.

His main concern was to stay well out of sight, which he did by crouching behind the bed, while through the space beneath the curtain he stared at the elaborately studded boots which were all he could see of the man who stood in the outer room talking roughly to the Ju family.

The boots were of blue velvet, studded with brass rivets, with thick rope soles. The heels carried spurs that came to a single long point. The boots were about the size that Casca would wear himself. The man's exceptional height was added to by the elaborate spiked knob atop his leather helmet. From his position Casca could hear a horse snorting and stamping outside in the street.

The visitor announced himself as the representative of the warlord Zhang Jintao who was visiting the village to consult with the community elders about circumstances in the countryside, and to exact tribute.

Casca heard Ju Liqun bleat that the insatiable tax-gatherers of the ever-hungry and heartless emperor had already taken everything of value.

The collector answered with grunts of disbelief and disinterest, and Liqun quickly abandoned his act and went

59

to the counter. He produced a small rosewood box and handed over the pile of coins that it contained.

The extortioner took the money with one hand while a backhand swing of the other arm swept Ju Liqun into a corner.

Songzhen ran to the most obvious of the family hoards, a broken teapot atop the stove. She brought it to the tax gatherer and emptied its coins into his outstretched hand.

As the last coin fell she was hurled to join her husband on the floor.

"Stupid people," the collector snarled, "do you think we can protect you from your enemies without money?"

He drew his heavy sword and pointed it at the children, who cowered against the wall.

"Look at this sword. It is all that stands between you and the greedy emperor and the even greedier foreign devils. Without our swords to protect you, you would have long since starved. And now you try to cheat us of our just stipends."

Sword in hand, he started for the room where Casca was hiding. As he moved past the sack curtain Songzhen's terrified shriek turned him for a moment, and he was just turning back when Casca's feet caught him in the chest as he came up from behind the bed and tumbled across its width, utilizing all the momentum of his somersault in the kick.

The extortioner went down backward and his sword clattered to the floor.

Casca sprang from the bed and hurled himself onto the fallen man.

But he was not there, and Casca crashed heavily to the floor. The big man kept rolling, then sprang to his feet, his retrieved sword in hand.

"Oh shit," Casca panted, rolling frantically in his turn

as the sword came down to cut deep into the floor where he had been.

"Ah-ha," the warrior shouted, "a foreign devil is harbored here. I will have some questions once I have killed him."

With confidence he moved closer. As he raised the sword Casca shouted: "Zhang Jintao will have your head if you harm me."

The warrior paused. His stupid little eyes looked worried. How could a barbarian know Zhang Jintao? It did not occur to him that Casca had just heard the name from his own lips. How could a barbarian speak Chinese?

"You know the warlord Zhang Jintao?"

Casca made a quick assessment of the man. A typical tax collector, pea-sized brain in a giant body. Easier to fight the brain while he could get away with it.

"Take me to him," Casca demanded imperiously.

"I will take him your head," the warrior replied and commenced to raise his sword again.

"And you will surely lose your own. I have a message for Zhang Jintao from the Baron Chung Wei."

Perfectly true, Casca thought to himself. I was Baron of Chung Wei under the Emperor Tzin. Sure, it was more than a thousand years ago, but I don't want to sow confusion and further addle this ape's head.

He smiled at the thought.

The tax gatherer was totally confused. Surely the barbarian was lying. But he could not risk his warlord's displeasure. And why was the foreign devil smiling? He motioned with his sword for Casca to precede him.

Casca stepped through the doorway and saw Deng Ziyang jerk the edge of his hand across his throat in the universal gesture.

His mind was racing as he tried to weigh his chances of escape once outside the house, or the even less likely chance of his being able to outwit the warlord once he met him. The old man's gesture decided him, and he turned back toward the warrior, who was just a pace behind him, the point of his sword a few inches from Casca.

Casca pointed to his satchel, noting as he did so that it had been moved.

"I have some valuables in this room," he said.

"Aha." The giant turned, and as he did Casca drew his knife and drove it into his kidneys with all his force, pushing the big man farther into the room.

He staggered and almost fell, but turned on his buckling knees and swung his heavy sword for Casca's throat.

But Casca had hung back. The sword missed, and Casca leaped forward to reach under the sword arm and drive his knife deep into the extortioner's heart. He pitched forward onto the floor, a comical look of amazement on his stupid face.

Deng Ziyang spoke from the doorway. "The only thing to do, or we were all dead. But now, my esteemed friend, we must move fast. We must hide the body of this stinking Korean, and his horse too."

"Korean?" Casca asked.

"Of course Korean. No Chinese is so big. Many warlords hire stupid Korean mercenaries as tax collectors. They hate Chinese anyway, so they are especially brutal to us."

The old man's voice had taken on a note of authority and evident enjoyment to be involved in some action.

Casca realized that Deng was also enjoying the prospect of recovering from the corpse not only the Ju family's money, but everything that the collector had extorted from the villagers that day. Many of the village families would recover their tax contributions—and reward Deng Ziyang for them.

Indeed, Liqun and Songzhen had already removed the

extortioner's belt and pouch, and were now busy taking off his clothes, while Deng Ziyang studied the contents of the pouch.

Casca picked up the shirt of heavy blue cotton and realized for the first time how lucky he had been with his two knife thrusts. The shirt was of two layers of cotton, lined with small scales of hardened leather to form a sort of armor to protect the wearer from sword slashes.

Casca's thrust to the kidneys had gone under the length of the shirt, and his second thrust had found one of the gaps between the leather scales.

He shrugged his way into the shirt and found it a tolerable, if rather tight fit. He added the leg pieces and the small apron made of the same material. He took the belt and pouch from Deng and smiled to see the old man's face fall, then light up as Casca emptied the pouch on the floor. There was a knife in a sheath on the right side of the belt, the sword scabbard on the left.

By now Ju had removed the studded boots and Casca stepped into them, the thick rope soles adding a couple of inches to his height. He put on the leather helmet and pulled the peak down over his eyes.

"Good enough to get by if I don't come face-to-face with any of the warlord's other men."

He crossed the small front room and went out into the street to look at the horse. It was a fine animal, in good condition, with a splendid saddle. A leather socket held a bamboo lance about eight feet long, and from the pommel hung a round cane shield and a face guard.

The guard was in the form of a mask, made of a number of small metal plates riveted together to resemble a man's face with eye slits, a nose pierce, and a hideously grinning mouth.

Casca went back into the Ju house. In the back room the naked body lay on the floor and Casca studied its bulk distastefully. Killing a man never troubled him, but he had an ingrained objection to the tedium of disposing of bodies. Especially when it had to be done in secret.

Dead bodies, he knew, were heavy; they stank; and they were almost impossible to carry unobserved even in the dark—if they were lucky enough to be able to wait for darkness.

While he was pondering the problem he saw Songzhen returning to the room with a broad-bladed Chinese cooking knife in her hand. Ju Liqun and Deng Ziyang struggled to turn the body onto its face, and she squatted beside it and began to slice through the backs of the knees. As she pushed the severed legs aside her husband wrapped them in pieces of sacking.

She wielded the cleaver like an ax to cut through the hip joints and then went to work at the shoulders, and lastly chopped through the neck. She carried out the whole operation as disinterestedly as she might have butchered a pig.

The rumble of iron wheels on cobblestones alerted Casca that Deng had brought his two-wheeled cart to the door, and he watched as the family carried out the sack-wrapped dismembered body and stowed the individual bundles under the grass and manure where he himself had hidden the previous day.

They carried out the task in full view of the people passing in the street. Much smarter than waiting for darkness, Casca thought.

But what was he to do with himself, and the horse?

CHAPTER NINE

"Where will you bury the body?" Casca asked Deng.

"Bury?"

"Well, what are you going to do with it?"

"Why, just dispose of it like any other garbage, of course."

"Of course. But where?"

"Anywhere. Here. There. What difference?"

"You mean you're just going to throw the bits about the countryside?"

Deng's puzzlement showed in his face. "What else?"

"Well, isn't that unhygienic?"

"Hygienic?"

The hell with it, Casca thought. What the hell do I care what they do with the bits. Aloud he said: "And the horse?"

Again Casca saw the look of bewilderment at his questions, which, for Deng, were not questions.

"Horses are to ride."

Goddammit, the old bastard's right.

As the idea registered Casca was already on his way. In a moment he was out in the street untying the horse's reins and vaulting into the saddle.

He paused just long enough to take the face guard from

the pommel and put it on. Then he dug his heels into the horse's flanks.

"Let's go, let's go. C'mon horse, we're getting out of here."

The horse reared slightly, then took off at a fast canter that carried Casca to the village gates before he had time to think more about it.

The startled gate guards made as if to run into the road. To leave the village any faster than a walk was a serious, punishable offense. Two more heavily armed men, whom Casca took to be part of the warlord's force, looked on amused.

One of the guards was moving, arm upraised, into the direct path of the horse, when some survival instinct alerted him that this horse and rider were not going to stop—for anything.

He stopped stock still where he was, and as Casca thundered by, he used his upraised arm to salute.

"Who was that?" his startled comrade asked.

"You want to know, you run after him," was the reply, and the two guards tacitly agreed to forget about the masked rider. So one of the warlord's men had left the village. So what? The sooner they all left, the better.

But Casca heard one of the other armed men laugh and shout to his comrade: "Hu Wei's in a hurry as usual."

Half a mile or so beyond the gates Casca slowed his mount to a comfortable canter.

The animal loped along with Casca enjoying the ride immensely. All around him the countryside unfolded. The road ran through groves of cypresses and teak trees. In what Europeans called the thirteenth century the great Kublai Khan, whose empire extended from the islands of the China Sea to Poland, had decreed that roads be planted with trees to provide shade in summer and covered with road markers for the benefit of travelers when the ground might be blanketed with snow. His edict had been followed ever since, for the astrologers told that those who plant trees are rewarded with long life.

Small green fields were intersected by shallow irrigation ditches. Peasants in blue smocks and cone-shaped hats were at work with draft animals. Low, steep mountains broke the sky in the near distance.

This was the road along which Casca had traveled from the river port of Tsungkow.

"Sure beats the cowshit express." He laughed heartily.

A new plan was formulating in his mind as he rode the long slope to a crest in the road. He would ride all the way to Tsungkow, where he would contact the Irish missionary priest who was the British consul's local intelligence agent. He would send a dispatch to Hong Kong that the situation had deteriorated drastically, that the village of Shou-Chang had been occupied by the warlord Zhang Jintao, and the people were hacking each other to pieces over involvement with foreign devils, and that he had barely escaped with his life by killing one of the warlord's men and fleeing on his horse.

The consul would readily believe this behavior of the Chinese and would accept Casca's assessment that all foreigners were now in grave danger and that all hell was about to break loose.

In Tsungkow he would sell the horse and saddle and Hu Wei's weapons and take a river boat to Chaochow to make his way eventually to Hong Kong.

And to hell with secrecy. The intelligence mission was over. Once in Tsungkow he would abandon all pretense and declare himself a British soldier and so claim the protection provided by the treaties. He would travel in luxury to Hong Kong, charging the queen of England with the expense, and the emperor of China with his protection.

What he got for the horse and arms and what he still had

in his pouch would nicely complement his sergeant's pay. And if the consul wanted to retrieve what he had cached at Ju Liqun's house, well, Casca would be happy to lead an armed force to the village of Shou-Chang to recover it.

There was going to be great strife between the village and Zhang Jintao over the disappearance of his tax collector, surely a sufficient uproar to satisfy the consul's predictions of dire troubles. And the appearance in the village of a British army force might well set off enough fireworks to ignite the whole countryside and get the consul the attention from Whitehall that he so earnestly craved.

Yes, Casca thought, it should all work out pretty nicely for me.

The thought was still running through his mind when he suddenly found himself flying through the air over the horse's head.

And when he came to alongside the horse, still struggling to rise on a broken leg, his last thought rolled through his mind again. But somehow this time it didn't seem to fit quite so neatly. There were all sorts of jagged edges to the idea, like the splintered pieces of bone he could now see showing through the flesh of his horse's leg.

And there seemed to be altogether too much noise.

Gradually the focus of Casca's mind cleared and he recalled the horse stumbling on the rutted roadway. Then he realized that he was not alone. Not at all alone, he discovered with a start as he recognized the noise as men's voices and the stamping of hooves, and saw the many horses' legs around where he lay in the road.

His horse snorted violently, then lay still, and Casca realized that one of the riders who surrounded him had driven a lance through its heart.

A painful throb started up in his head, and another in his left wrist. Through the pain, the voices that he could hear started to become clear.

His eyes roved over the horses and riders before him. They were almost identical with the imperial knights who had greeted him at the Jade Gate on his first visit to China in the time of the Roman Emperor Nero.

The horses' heads and necks were protected by padded silk. Gilded rivet heads told Casca that the silk was lined with interlocking metal plates. The saddle flaps, great disks of studded leather, protected the flanks, and a padded silk crupper covered the hind parts. The bridles were of leather, ornamented and protected with numerous tiny lacquered metal shields. The riders' gloves were of the same material, three shields to each finger, a dozen or so on the back of the hand, and more on the cuffs, which extended up the arms over the sleeves of armored shirts.

One rider was covered from neck to ankle in gold brocade embroidered in green and edged with black velvet. Hundreds of gilt rivet heads studded the brocade, securing the metal lining plates, and there were shoulder pieces in the shape of gilded dragons. His iron helmet was decorated with raised scrolls of gold, set with ruby, turquoise, and pink coral. Casca recalled that this indicated that he was an imperial baron, an official of the second class.

No mean thing to be a baron, even second class, thought Casca, who had once been one. There were only twelve thousand of them in all of China.

A long lance rested in a leather socket, beside it a round shield of studded leather, and a huge bow, the back of which was of horn, the ends bound in sharkskin. Casca remembered these bows, much larger than anything ever used in Europe, with an immensely heavy pull, extraordinary considering the small size of the archers. The quiver held many arrows, most of them about three feet long with heavy iron heads.

There was only one modern touch—the gun that hung in a holster alongside the lance.

The gun barrel was about five feet long, but it ended in a pistol grip that would surely need two hands to hold. The end of the barrel was exposed, and there seemed to be no sight, but Casca could see that it was inlaid with flowers in gold and silver for its entire length.

A weapon or an ornament? he wondered.

"You're sure he's one of Zhang Jintao's extortioners?"

"The worst of them, Baron Ying. His size is unmistakable, and we have many reports of that fiendish mask and that huge body in action. He's a foul animal. Not Chinese, thank the gods."

"What is he then?"

"Don't know. I've never seen his face. Some who have say he's Korean."

"Well, let's have a look."

There was a creaking of leather as one of the riders dismounted and the mask was jerked down from Casca's face.

"Blue eyes! Does Zhang have a British devil for his tax collector?"

Casca looked around him. He tried to rise, but when he put his weight on his hands immense pain shot through his left wrist, taking his breath away.

He struggled to his feet. What the hell to say?

"Greetings, noble baron," he said to the man he took to be the leader.

"Silence, dog," the leader snapped. He motioned to the man standing beside Casca. He went to his horse and returned with a long leather whip.

Fire seared through Casca's neck as the thong wound around it. He grabbed the thong and tugged, yanking the man off-balance and pulling him toward him. With his good hand he clubbed him on the neck, knocking him to the ground. He drew his sword and backed away.

One man on foot, four men on horseback. Not good odds, but the only odds going.

With his left hand Casca tried to unbuckle Hu's heavy sword belt. If he could get his Webley in his hand he could adjust the odds a little more favorably. It might be small and the barrel lack ornament, but he would back it against the baron's giant pistol.

But his injured left hand made no impression on the heavy buckle.

The leader looked at him in some amusement.

"The dog has some spirit, anyway." He drew his lance and pointed it at Casca's chest. The other three riders drew their weapons and moved their horses to surround him, while the man he had felled got to his feet and faced him, sword in hand.

"Put down your sword," the leader said. "You are our prisoner."

"I prefer to die here," Casca answered, and slashed at the man on foot, who parried the blow skillfully and lunged at Caca. The mounted men looked on as they fought.

"But we are not going to kill you." The leader spoke easily. "We have need of what you can tell us, and you are going to tell us."

Torture had never been a strong point with Casca. He hated to have to suffer it, didn't even care to inflict it. Better to die on the sword.

But then he felt the jab of a lance at his back, not quite heavy enough to pierce his leather armor.

He swung to face the horseman just in time to parry another thrust of the lance.

From behind a sword struck him on the shoulder, and again his armor saved him a cut. But the next lance thrust from behind found a gap in the leather scales over his shoulder blade and he felt a spasm of pain shoot through his right arm, almost enough to make him drop the sword.

He swung the heavy sword in a furious arc and drove back all of his attackers. He continued to swing the weapon in a figure eight, turning all the time so that none of the attackers came close.

Indeed they didn't try. They watched in amusement and waited for him to tire.

It wouldn't be too long, Casca realized as he felt warm blood oozing from his wounded back. He leaped at the man on foot, aiming a downswing of the blade at his head.

But the man retreated, then riposted skillfully, forcing Casca to yield ground—to back into another lance and collect a wound in the buttock. He started forward only to be met by the skillful swordsman and be driven back onto the lance again.

Then another lance pinked him in the arm and the sword fell from his grasp.

Before he could reach for it the swordsman was standing over it.

In furious humiliation Casca drew Hu's knife and charged at the baron, intent on dragging him from his horse and killing him or being killed in the attempt.

But the swinging shaft of another rider's lance caught him in the throat and stopped him in mid-rush.

He opened his hand so that the knife lay on his palm and swung overarm to hurl the knife at the baron's throat. But his wounds sent a spasm through the arm as he threw, and the knife went wild.

He stood glowering, four lances and a sword pointed at him.

The hell with it. He wasn't about to run onto a lance. He didn't intend to suffer an agonizing death from which he knew he would come back to life.

He sat on the ground and went back to trying to unbuckle Hu's sword belt so that he could get at his pistol.

"Well," the one who had identified him, said, "you're

made of better material than your reputation would suggest. I understood your specialty to be fighting women and old men.''

''I am not who you think I am.''

''Then get up,'' the baron said, ''and we will learn who you are.''

.Casca seethed. He cursed the Nazarene, whose curse deprived him of the dignity of an honorable death.

''Which way?'' he spat from his position on the ground.

The baron gestured with his lance. ''To Shou-Chang, where I believe we will find your master Zhang Jintao and his horde.''

''I do not know this Zhang,'' Casca said, ''but I doubt that five men can defeat his forces.''

The baron smiled and socketed his lance. He waved his arm and pointed toward Shou-Chang. Casca heard the movement of many men, and a small army appeared on the road at the crest of the hill where they had been resting amongst the trees that fringed the road.

''Get up, dog,'' the leader repeated, ''we have need of your information.''

Well, he wasn't finished yet.

The whip that had been wound around his neck now lay on the ground beside him. He snatched it up and came to his feet, flailing it about, taking out the swordsman's eye, and lashing the mounted horses so that they bolted away with their riders struggling to control them.

He leaped into the one empty saddle and hammered his heels into the horse's flanks, racing down the road past two of the riders who were just succeeding in bringing their mounts under control.

The flailing whip caught one horse in the throat and it reared and threw the rider. The other he lashed on the rump and it broke into a wild gallop, crashing through the trees that lined the roadside to fall heavily into an irrigation ditch.

Three thoughts suddenly came to Casca. All bad.

His left wrist, which he had used to haul himself into the saddle and to hold the reins, was now aching horribly and he could feel the fingers growing numb.

His right arm, thanks to the wound in his shoulder blade and the other in the arm, was now also a throbbing agony, and he could scarcely hold on to the whip.

Worst of all—he was going the wrong way.

His heels were still raking the horse's sides with his spurs, the animal giving its all as it galloped toward Shou Chang, where the warlord Zhang and his troops waited. And they would scarcely welcome the man who had slain and robbed their tax collector.

And behind him were the five nobles he had escaped, and behind them their small army. There was nothing for it but to keep going.

Well, at least the gate guards would not stand in his way.

They didn't.

They saw him coming from a distance, and Casca's fast clouding senses were just sufficient enough for him to remember to pull up the face guard.

The gate guards stood carefully aside as he raced through the portal. The warlord's two men laughed uproariously: "That's Hu Wei. Always in a hurry."

In spite of his wounds Casca laughed. Another few moments and they would be in something of a hurry themselves.

But, by the great balls of Mars, what the fuck was he going to do now?

As if in answer, Deng Ziyang chose that moment to haul his cart into the road.

Casca tried to wheel his horse, but in the narrow street there was nowhere to go, and no space to stop.

He tried desperately to will the horse to jump the width of the small cart as he had often seen cowboys do in America, but neither he nor the horse knew how.

The horse's chest struck the cart at full gallop, smashing and overturning it, and strewing its load of grass and cowshit and dismembered body pieces along the street, with Casca tumbling among the mess.

The impact wrenched the crossbar of the shafts from Deng's grasp, leaving him standing. The shrewd old man appraised the circumstances in an instant and slipped quickly through the open doorway into Ju Liqun's store.

He was already moving before he saw the great warlord Zhang approaching from the other end of the street, but this appearance hurried him, and he was quick to close and bar the door behind him, motioning to his daughter's family to be quiet while herding them into the back room where all five of them huddled in the farthest corner.

Zhang and his entourage were startled by the noise of the crash and were astonished to see what appeared to be Hu Wei flying through the air, accompanied by a number of sackcloth bundles which came apart in their flight to reveal the same Hu Wei's head, as well as his arms and legs and trunk. The horse was screaming shrilly, its chest impaled on the iron boss of the wheel, its belly punctured by several pieces of broken wood, the blue bag of its intestines oozing out.

Zhang and his men came to a halt.

Two Hu Weis?

Zhang was not a man to worry easily, but he was highly superstitious. It had never occurred to him that his tax gatherer might have two heads, but now it seemed that he had, and a whole lot of other spare parts as well.

CHAPTER TEN

Casca came to, lying on his stomach, to find himself looking into the mad eyes of Hu Wei, staring at him out of the dead head that sat before him in the roadway.

He tried to rise, but neither of his arms would take his weight. He rolled onto his back and sat up.

Beyond the city gates he could see an approaching cloud of dust. Horses. He began to remember and realized that these were his pursuers. And that he owed one of them an eye.

He swiveled on his rump and saw that the other end of the narrow street was blocked at the turn by another band of horsemen, whom he rightly took to be the warlord Zhang Jintao and his cohort.

"Jupiter's fat ass," he cursed, "what a busy fucking town."

"Hu Wei," the warlord called from where he sat astride his horse. "Why do you have two heads today?"

"By the two-headed dog, Janus, who guards the way to Hades, I'll show you," Casca muttered as he picked up Hu's head. He reversed it and rammed it hard onto the ornamented spike atop his helmet.

Groggily, he got to his feet, turning as he did to look back along the road.

A babble of excited and apprehensive shouts broke from Zhang's men as they saw what they took to be their comrade in arms with his back to them, while his head glared at them from above his helmet.

The thrust of the spike had set off some nervous response, and the eyes were blinking rapidly, the tongue vibrating in the open mouth.

Everywhere along the street doors were slamming shut, bars falling into place.

The pursuing horsemen were now slowing to approach the gates at a walk to comply with the established protocol. Nobles of the imperial court would not set a bad example merely to pursue a malefactor.

And Baron Ying Ruochen and his lieutenants had another reason to slow their pace.

Casca had turned back to face the warlord, and they could now see Hu Wei's writhing head. It was much more animated than the iron mask they had been looking at a moment earlier.

Zhang, for his part, felt more comfortable looking at the mask and the back of Hu's head, even though the Korean's long black hair hung down over the forehead of the mask and lent it the look of a live face.

"Er, Hu Wei," Zhang asked respectfully, "who are these horsemen who pursue you?"

Casca swung around to glance toward the gates, then back to Zhang. The effect, as Hu's head wobbled on the spike and his hair swayed about above the mask, was to make both heads look very much alive.

The approaching army was still not out of sight around the turn in the road. Good. And the nobles were still too far away from where Zhang sat astride his horse for him to perceive who they were. Best of all the men whose eye Casca had taken was not with them, no doubt staying along the road to have his wound tended.

"Some rich merchants whom I tried to rob. But they are well armed and they drove me off, but now we can take them and their gold."

Zhang well knew Hu to be a coward, and this story rang true. He still felt uncomfortable about the two heads, but it was not too bad looking at the mask. And the mention of gold removed his last reservation.

He spurred his horse forward, thinking to attack the merchants, and his men moved too. But at that moment the two men he had posted by the gate heard Ying Ruochen identify himself as Baron of Chaochow, and at the same time they saw the first ranks of the baron's army round the turn in the road.

Shouting warnings, they started to run toward Zhang, but were brought up short by the grisly sight of the two-headed monster. They faltered and turned, to be cut down by the swords of the baron's lieutenants.

Zhang was spurring his horse forward, when he, too, saw the approaching army.

He pulled his horse up short a little distance from where Casca stood by the upturned cart and his dying horse.

"Hu Wei," Zhang shouted in some confusion, "do you lie to me?"

Realizing his ruse hadn't worked, he answered, "Alas master, this spare head is not reliable."

Zhang lost interest in the explanation as he saw the nobles urging their horses forward. He wheeled his horse around, colliding with the press of horses and men behind him. His front ranks tried to turn too, and, in turn, crashed into those behind them. Farther back, Zhang's troops were still pressing forward, every man anxious to be among the first to fall upon the rich merchants. The narrow street was jammed with wheeling horses and men trying to draw their weapons as they began to realize their situation.

The nobles were now almost to where the upturned cart

blocked the street, alongside the two-headed monster and his horse.

Casca's aching fingers had made no progress with Hu's heavy sword belt, and his revolver remained out of his reach under the armored jacket.

As the nobles reached him, he took Hu's head from his helmet and hurled it into the milling mass of the warlord's men. Then he crawled into the space between the cart and the wall where he could not be too easily reached. The nobles moved one by one through the narrow gap at the other end of the cart, ignoring him for the moment, being much more interested in coming to grips with the warlord and his men.

The flying head struck Zhang on the shoulder, ricocheted up into the air, and came down again amongst his ranks. Everywhere horses shied and men cringed away from it. They were still in complete disarray when the nobles' lances spitted the first of them.

Now Zhang's men had to turn again to defend themselves, and the baron and his lieutenants were able to hack them to pieces as they tried to maneuver in the narrow space.

Then the rest of the army was upon them, and the cobblestones ran thick with blood. The air rang with the clash of swords. Dying men screamed, horses neighed as their hooves slipped on the bloodied stones.

Zhang's men broke and fled, but the baron's men were close behind them and made great sport of cutting them down from behind with their swords or running them through with their lances.

The rout moved around the corner, the shouts and screams moved away, and Casca found himself alone in the street outside Ju Liqun's store.

He scraped gently at the door.

"Deng Ziyang," he called, "the battle is over. It is safe now. Let me in. I will reward you well."

Inside the Ju household the cowering family heard Casca's repeated calls and argued amongst themselves.

"We have had enough trouble," Ju Liqun whined. "Let him die in the street."

"Stupid fool," Deng hissed at him, "how much trouble is enough? What do you know of enough who never has enough to drink? And whose children never have enough to eat. Do you not yet know that one man's trouble is another man's opportunity? And is it not the way of the Hakka to assist strangers and so acquire merit in the eyes of the gods. Let him in, I say, and you may yet be rich."

"We already have the barbarian's boxes," Ju Liqun argued. "Surely when we break them open we shall be rich enough."

"And how rich is rich enough? And how do you know what might be in the boxes? We know the barbarian has money on his person. And when your kitchen god, Tsou Shen, reports on this household for the year, shall he speak well or ill of your hospitality? Let him in, I say."

They were still arguing when the baron's army came back around the corner with Zhang Jintao's head and several others on their lances, and a number of prisoners being dragged along with ropes around their necks.

Casca groaned at the sight. In another moment he was looking into the points of a dozen lances and swords. Wearily he got to his feet and came out from behind the cart. A noose dropped over his head and he was dragged along the street with the other prisoners. They were taken to the village square where their captors beat upon wooden drums to summon the population.

The baron and his lieutenants were joined by the elders of the village and the headman and his men. The Buddhist priests didn't come to the square, but sat on the temple steps to watch.

One by one the prisoners were paraded and villagers

who had suffered at their hands gave evidence against them. As the evidence against each one came to an end Baron Ying asked the prisoner if he had anything to say in his defense.

Most of the prisoners remained mute and were beheaded on the spot. A few denied the charges and were beheaded anyway. Some burst into tears and begged for mercy, and these were summarily beheaded, too. Some only had a few accusers and their crimes only amounted to pilfering, and these had one or both hands chopped off, the bleeding stumps being cauterized with flaming torches and then plunged into a barrel of hot pitch.

Casca noticed that as the trials proceeded the villagers became more courageous in coming forward with evidence, and soon they were competing with each other to establish the evildoing of the prisoners. The last few men were vehemently accused of every possible crime, and, although it seemed clear that the villagers were now inventing their evidence, they were beheaded anyway.

At last Casca was the only prisoner left.

He was dragged to the center of the square to the boos and hisses of the population. Villager after villager told of how this huge beast in the hideous mask had looted their homes, raped their wives and daughters, killed their sons.

But there was a sudden silence when the mask was jerked down from his face. Several people who had been loud in their accusations qualified before the steady gaze of Casca's blue eyes. A number withdrew and hid amongst the crowd. A hush fell over the square. Even the sobbing and groaning of the mutilated ceased.

"Who knows this man?" the baron asked, but nobody spoke.

He singled out one villager who had been loud in his accusations and who had stood his ground when the mask was removed.

"Is this the man?" the baron demanded.

"No, Lord, he is not. The beast who raped my daughter and killed my young son had black eyes and skin the color of my own."

One by one other accusers confirmed his statement.

"Very well," the baron said at last, "we will interrogate this strange one and allow him to accuse himself." He gave a signal and Casca's guard jerked at the rope around his neck. Another tied his hands, forcing a scream from him as the rope wrenched at his broken wrist.

The baron gave some of the captured weapons and horses to the village. Only a handful of the baron's men had been wounded, and these were placed on carts borrowed from the villiage. There was no such humane treatment for Casca, but he was allowed to mount one of the captured horses.

The army moved out of the village and headed back along the road to Tsungkow, dragging Casca along behind them by the rope around his neck. He suffered mightily on the thirty-mile ride. None of his wounds was deep, and he was no longer losing much blood, but every stride of his horse jolted his wounded butt on the saddle so that he came to think of his earlier ride in Deng's cart as a luxurious excursion.

When they arrived at last in Tsungkow Casca was taken to the town jail and handed over to the turnkey, who removed Hu's sword belt and then untied Casca's hands so that he could remove the armored shirt. He gleefully seized Casca's knife, but was puzzled by the revolver.

"It is a powerful weapon," Casca told him. "More powerful than the large handgun the baron carries. But it can be easily damaged, and if you do damage it the baron will punish you severely."

The turnkey had seen a few handguns, but had never

seen one in use. He grasped the Webley by the pistol grip, pointed it in Casca's direction, and pulled the trigger.

Casca threw himself to the floor and the shot went into the stone wall. The jailer dropped the gun in alarm.

Casca seized it and pointed it at his fat belly. He backed away in terror. Casca could hear feet running to report this phenomenon.

He backed the jailer against the wall and slammed him in the temple with the gun butt. He pitched to the floor and Casca picked up his heavy key ring and threw it through the bars of one of the cells.

He retrieved his knife and held the hilt in his teeth while he hacked through the rope on his wrists. He put on Hu Wei's shirt again, this time with his gun belt outside. As he ran from the jail he could hear the prisoners opening one cell after another. Good. A mass jailbreak should slow any pursuit.

As Casca reached the courtyard that separated the jail from the town's administrative buildings he saw an under-jailer and an important-looking official running for the prison.

He took his time and shot the official neatly through the head. The terrified under-jailer fell begging to his knees and Casca walked over to him and clubbed him senseless.

There were numerous horses in the adjoining stable yard, some of them still saddled. Casca grabbed the nearest one and managed painfully to get into the saddle. He kicked the horse into a gallop and raced away.

He gritted his teeth in agony. His left hand was now just a ball of pain. He could not use it to hold the reins and had wound them around his fist, which didn't give him much control over the horse, but he didn't need all that much control. He didn't care where the animal went so long as it moved fast, and his pointed spurs saw to that.

His right arm ached from the wound in his back to the

wound in his arm, to the fingers that held his revolver. And he felt the wounds in his rump open afresh.

A pikeman appeared in his path, his weapon pointed directly at Casca's gut, the man resolutely standing his ground as the distance between them diminished.

Casca held out his throbbing right arm and, pointing along the length of the pike, pulled the trigger.

The man went over backward, a bullet in his heart, his weapon sticking straight up in the air.

He died in an instant and his hand released the pike, which fell forward to take Casca's horse squarely in the chest, the butt of the weapon being braced against the man's dead body and the ground. The weight and speed of horse and rider ran the pike deep into the horse's body and it crashed to its knees.

As he flew into the air one more time, Casca thought: "That's the third fucking horse I've lost today—so far."

CHAPTER ELEVEN

"He lives."

Casca heard a voice that he thought he could recall from somewhere.

"Ah, yes," another voice said, "he is not badly hurt."

In an aching fury Casca forced his eyes open to see who this was who decided he wasn't badly hurt. Not badly hurt? he thought. I am hurt almost unto death.

An elderly Chinese squatted beside him where he lay naked on a bench. The walls of the room were covered with what appeared to be anatomy charts. The old man was manipulating a long silver needle that was inserted in the right side of Casca's neck.

A great weariness assailed him and he swooned back toward oblivion. Consciousness hurt. Casca tried to avoid it, seeking the darkness where the pain was blurred, if not softened.

But the doctor pushed the needle deeper, and spun its shaft between his palms. Deep within him Casca felt a tingling that spread throughout his body, gradually replacing the pain.

His head cleared and he felt the pain diminishing as the doctor continued to twirl the length of the needle. Against his will his eyes opened again.

Baron Ying—so it was his voice he had heard—stood over him. The baron spoke.

"For now you are going to live, Hu Wei, or whatever your name is. We will know presently, and then I will think on your punishment."

"I am not Hu Wei. My name is Cas-Ca Sho."

"Sho? Long life? Then you are wrongly named. You have not yet had a long life, and I assure you, you are not going to live much longer."

In spite of his predicament Casca chuckled faintly as he looked up at the baron.

"I have already lived longer than you could dream, Baron, and I will yet outlive you and your grandchildren— and their grandchildren."

The baron looked at him in some puzzlement.

"You talk in riddles, Cas-Ca Sho. But you have cost me many men today. And you will pay for those with your life—after I have learned from you what I need to know."

He turned to leave, saying to the doctor over his shoulder, "Poon Fong, kindly let me know when he is strong enough for questioning."

Casca could feel his body rebuilding itself even faster than he had ever previously experienced as the old doctor worked on him with the silver needle. His broken wrist had been set and bandaged, and the pain from his arm, as if the bones were slowly breaking apart, came, he knew, from the reverse process of the bones putting themselves back together. But, never since the curse of Jesus had first caused his body to go through this process, had it happened so fast.

The pain was already diminishing; the swelling was noticeably reduced. And Casca was feeling stronger and stronger by the minute.

The doctor removed the long needle and moved to insert it in another position.

Casca didn't intend to wait around to be tortured. Now was the time to go, or never.

He came up quickly from the bench, his right hand moving for the doctor's neck to immobilize him.

But Poon Fong wasn't there. He had swayed just out of Casca's reach, and as Casca's fingers closed on air the doctor struck him in the throat with the tips of two fingers, knocking him back onto the bench, gasping for air. Without speaking the doctor inserted the needle in the new place as if nothing had happened.

Casca lay quiet, recovering and thinking. Clearly the old man had been studying the way of the open hand as long as he had studied medicine. So, he was going to be a tougher nut than Casca had reckoned on. But then, Casca could be a lot tougher, too. He put aside the thought that this Fong might match him at his best. After all, he had not lived one-tenth as long as Casca had, and Casca had devoted much time to the way of the open hand since the sage Lao-tze first introduced him to the philosophy and practice of K'ung Fu-tzu, the wise man Marco Polo had called Confucius in Latin.

But now the old man was using the needle differently, tapping gently on its head, each tap sending a pleasant tingle through Casca's body, and even through his mind. The urgency of his need to escape, the fear of his impending torture, receded into the pleasant glow that was enveloping him. Even the mental torture of the prophet's curse that rarely left his mind, while awake or asleep, slipped away from him, and his consciousness faded into a quiet sleep.

He awoke refreshed, alert, and hungry. He tried to sit up, but found that he was restrained.

His head was wedged in a wooden block and a leather strap across his eyes and nose prevented any movement of his head; a broad leather strap secured his arms and chest to the bench, and another strap secured his legs.

He heard a movement beside the bench, then footsteps leaving the chamber.

Well, dammit, he thought, I'm alive, and I feel much better. But I guess there's some sort of rough time coming.

He heard returning footsteps and guessed two men. He heard Baron Ying's voice: "Well, Hu Wei or Cas-Ca Sho, or whatever you care to call yourself, do you care to talk to us?"

"I do not like to be tortured, and if I could think of something that might interest you, I would tell it freely. My name I have already told you. I went to Shou-Chang village to sell silks and satins and ran into trouble with Zhang Jintao's tax collector and had to kill him. My horse stumbled while I was escaping, and it seems you arrived while I was unconscious. What else can I tell you?"

"Something true would be satisfactory. I have known many merchants who lie as stupidly as you do, but I have never known one to fight as well.

"Be warned, big man. Our method of interrogation never fails. But those who resist too long suffer permanently impaired minds.

"Start the treatment, Tian Yuanlong. Call me when he starts to babble."

Footsteps receded. Casca sensed that the man he had called Tian had stayed beside the bench. He could hear him doing something above his head.

Babble? Why should I start to babble? Casca wondered. So I can't move. Well, I can stand that. I can stand that forever. He closed his eyes under the strap and concentrated on emptying his mind of all thoughts and sensations so that he might enjoy this confinement, even profit from it.

A drop of water struck him on the forehead.

Damned nuisance, he thought. Is there condensation dripping from the ceiling? Did they move me to a dungeon while I slept?

Another drop seemed to confirm this idea, and Casca's mind shrugged. Not important. He renewed his concentration.

But transcendence eluded him. He could not empty his mind. The drops of water fell intermittently, each one jolting him back to an awareness of the strap across his eyes, of his confinement, of his captivity. He would determinedly put all of this away from him, focusing his closed eyes inward, concentrating all of his being on the single point between his eyebrows, the location of the third eye that looked into the mystic realm.

Which was exactly where these damned drops were hitting.

Not a coincidence. The thought came to him strikingly. Not a casual accident. Wherever the drops came from, he had been carefully placed so as to receive them at just this point.

Chinese water torture.

Well, so what? I can stand a little rain. I can stand this forever. He spoke aloud to the person beside the bench. "Can I have some water?"

"Of course." He had not heard the voice before. So the tough old doctor had been replaced by some sort of torturer. Well, the voice was pleasant enough.

He felt a cup at his lips and sipped a little water, then resettled his mind to handle the small problem of the drops falling on his forehead.

Hours passed and Casca was almost enjoying the game. The drops came not quite regularly, defying all Casca's attempts to count the time interval. Well, it made the game more interesting. Regular drops would have bored him unmercifully.

His torturer sat immobile beside him, breathing quietly, making no attempt to question or worry him.

"One, two, three, four, five, six . . ." *Splat*. "So,

that one was early. Two, three, four, five, six, seven, eight . . ." *Splat*. "Ah-ha. One, two, three, four, five, six, seven, where is it? nine, where . . ." *Splat*. "Okay, one, two, three, four, five . . ." *Splat*. "Real early that time. Two, three, four, five, six, seven, eight, nine, come on, ten . . ." *Splat*. "Of course. Two, three . . ."

Casca continued the count. It ceased to be amusing, but there was nothing else to do. Perhaps he could bait his jailer?

"You think this crap is going to make me talk?"

"Of course."

"Horseshit. I can take this forever."

"Really?" The voice was interested.

"Sure I can. What's the theory behind this torture anyway?"

"No theory. Only practice. Everybody talks."

"Well, meet the first who doesn't. Oh, and by the way, I don't have anything to tell."

"Not important. Many think they have nothing to tell."

Then he heard the footsteps leaving the room and he was left alone.

"One, two, three, four, five, six, seven, where is it? nine, ten, eleven, oh come on, twelve . . ." *Splat*. "One, two, three, four, five . . ." *Splat*. "What a stupid game. Three, four, five, six, seven, eight, nine, come on dammit, eleven, what no drop? thirteen . . ." *Splat*. "One, two, three . . ." *Splat*. "One, two, three, four, five, six, no drop? eight, nine, not yet? eleven, twelve, longest yet, fourteen . . ." *Splat*.

The sound of the returning footsteps was welcome. He heard the baron's voice: "Has he said anything of interest?"

And the answer: "Soon now."

Soon? Not likely, Casca thought.

He heard the scraping of wood on stone and guessed the two men had sat down, but neither of them spoke.

"Six, seven, eight, can't be much longer, ten, eleven, where's that drop? thirteen, fourteen, fifteen, sixteen, what?" *Splat.*

"One, two, three—listen to me you dumb bastards. This primitive fucking crap is not going to work on Casca Rufio Longinus. Let me tell you, you're not going to get one fucking word out of me. You hear me? Not one . . ." *Splat.*

"Okay, where were we? Three, four, five, six—if you think I could withstand Torquemada's rack and can't stand a little water . . ." *Splat.*

The baron spoke quietly. "Leave us now, Tian. I would hear his confessions alone." Casca heard the other man leave.

"One, two, three, four, five, six—if you imagine this is tough, you've never done cookhouse fatigue in the British army. Or a full-dress ceremonial parade in the noon sun. Or . . ." *Splat.*

"Doesn't this fucking water ever stop!?" The scream sounded strange in Casca's ears. Was it his own voice? He went determinedly back to his count.

"Five, six, seven, eight—let me tell you, this isn't torture, this is just fucking boredom, twelve, their—" *Splat.*

"One, two, three—if you keep me here for a month, I've got nothing to tell you. What is there to tell? The British are worried about an uprising. That's hardly news to you. The consul . . ." *Splat.*

"Fuck. Two, three, four, five—and another thing, if I babbled my head off for days, it wouldn't help you. If I told you the truth about myself, you simply wouldn't believe . . ." *Splat.*

"Stop that fucking water." His screech seemed to come right out of the top of his head.

"Don't think it's getting to me. I took more punishment

in the Roman legions for having an untidy bunk. This water crap is only a minor nuisance. Look at the scars on my thumbs . . ." *Splat*.

"Oh, shit. Three, four, five, six, I'm not going to break, nine, ten, don't care if it never comes, thirteen, four—" *Splat*.

"Okay. One, two, three . . ."

The baron sat impassively while Casca resolutely counted away the seconds between the drops. He neither questioned him nor spoke at all, nor answered Casca's attempts to provoke him into conversation until Casca suddenly shouted: *"Nunco Deco nihil, not correct."*

"Eras, not correct," said the baron, and the conversation continued in that Latin.

The baron sat and listened, only speaking quietly in Latin when Casca spoke in that language.

Casca told of his early life, his time in the Roman legions, and of the day on Golgotha when he put the Jewish guru out of his last misery. The stunned baron heard the dying Christ's curse and understood why Casca had adopted the name Sho—long life. Now, for the first time, Ying could understand how one body could have collected Casca's multitude of scars.

Then Casca's ravings changed to languages that the Cambridge-educated baron recognized but did not speak— Norse and German. Then Casca spoke for a long time in Chinese, then Japanese, then in the strange, guttural tongue of the Aztecs, then the harsh, percussive Mayan language.

Hours passed and Casca talked on. He spoke in French and in Spanish and in some of the melodic lilts of the South Pacific.

At last, at the end of many more hours, he was speaking in English and detailing his arrival in China, his execution of the lieutenant for the murder of Fei Jiyun, and his present assignment as spy.

It was some time before Casca realized that the drops had ceased. The strap was removed from his eyes, his head was gently freed from the restraining block, and he saw Ying removing the goatskin water bag that had been suspended above his head.

Casca had no urgent inclination to move. He felt drained.

The baron spoke quietly.

"You have told me much, ancient one. And what you have told me has very much changed my opinion of you. I am very pleased that I spared your life." He smiled. "Just as I am pleased that you didn't succeed in taking mine. I regret that you made it necessary for me to torture you to make you reveal your true history.

"The minds of some men recover from the water treatment. I hope you are such a one—for your own sake, and for mine. There is much use I could make of your talents, and in an enterprise that would reward you well.

"You impress me as an honest man, or as close to one as one ever finds. Certainly you are a capable man. And I see that you are no real enemy of my people, although you are in the army of the foreign devils.

"I hope we may yet work together."

He turned and left the chamber. Casca lay and looked at the stone ceiling.

What the hell did he mean? He could not remember anything since the commencement of the water treatment. He certainly couldn't remember telling anything.

He tried to recall what he might have told him, but his mind remained a blank. He could remember no more than what the baron had just told him. He was in China in the pay of the British army.

And there was somewhere in his mind the memory of a voice saying that he should remain always a soldier.

He stared at the stone ceiling and wondered.

CHAPTER TWELVE

The door opened, but Casca heard only the lightest of footfalls. He turned his head to see a tiny nun in a black habit and a coif. Only her face and hands showed. One hand carried a feather duster.

She came to the bench and peered down at Casca through thick pebble spectacles.

"Have you escaped us, you fiend?" she scowled at him.

Casca smiled at her concentrated malevolence.

"Escaped?"

"Well, you can talk anyway. Can you think, I wonder?"

Casca stared up at her. Think? About what?

"I think you're a nun. A Christian nun."

He felt faintly pleased, but also disturbed. He couldn't quite think what a nun was, or a Christian.

Something to do with a teacher called Christ. And Christ had something to do with his being a soldier.

"Oh, Christ," he muttered aloud.

Swish. The cane handle of the feather duster came down across his face, making him yelp in pain.

"Don't you take the name of the Lord in vain, you swine."

"Oh, my God," Casca groaned and earned another cruel

97

slash with the cane. This one caught him across the chest, but it still hurt.

"Hey, take it easy with that thing, Sister."

"What? Does the Roman executioner beg for mercy? You showed none to the Lamb of God."

What the hell is this old broad talking about? Roman? Executioner? Who does she think I am?

Then a surge of panic.

Who am I? Where am I?

He could feel a thousand thoughts trying to make themselves felt, but out of the conflict he could only isolate a few unrelated specks of memory.

A fall from a horse. An elegant Chinese. A comic image of a man at the end of a rope flapping about like a bird. A man on a cross . . .

"Jesus."

Another swish of the cane and Casca yelled again. "Hey, hold it there, Sister. What the hell are you doing? Just who do you think I am?"

"I know who you are. I don't know what you call yourself, but I know you, Casca Rufio Longinus, torturer of the Son of God. Accursed to soldier forever."

So I'm a soldier. But I think I'm in the British army. And it's a hell of a long time since Christ died. So how old am I?

The nun's face came nearer. She stared into Casca's eyes, concern showing on her face.

"Then you have lost your mind? You have escaped us—and the curse."

More confused flashes of memory came to Casca. Women. Lots of women. They came rolling through his mind in rapid succession like strumpets tumbling together in a bed.

And fighting. Fighting, fighting, fighting. He saw in his mind's eye one enemy after another. This one wielding a great ax, this one on horseback with a long lance, a horde of tribesmen with spears and shields, a giant with a huge, two-handed sword. And all of them dying. Dying on his sword, his knife, between his hands.

Then came flashes of himself being hacked open with an ax, run through with a sword, being strangled, a hand chopped off.

He felt pain in his left wrist. He remembered the mad eyes of the man who had hacked off his hand. The same mad eyes as this nun.

"Dacort!"

"Aha! So you remember Dacort."

Do I? Casca wondered. He had somehow recalled the name, as he remembered losing his hand, and his mutilator's crazy face. But that was all.

He lifted his head and could just see his bandaged wrist with the hand intact. And functioning, he was relieved to see as he moved the fingers.

But all else was confusion. Perhaps this crazy nun can tell me.

But the nun had fallen to her knees, and was prattling some sort of prayer: "Oh, Blessed Lamb, is this the end of all our hopes? If this hulking body no longer has a mind, is not Your curse at an end? How shall the Brotherhood of the Lamb now find You when You come again?"

Brotherhood of the Lamb? Casca remembered a sort of religious ceremony when the Elder Dacort had taken his hand.

But he could not connect the recollection into any web of memory.

The nun had come to the end of her lament and was standing beside the bench.

"Can a woman belong to a brotherhood?"

The nun struck him again.

"I am a nun. I am handmaiden to the brotherhood, as I am to the Church."

"And this brotherhood? What have these men to do with me?"

The feather duster fell again.

"They are not men, not filthy, lecherous monsters like you. They are sanctified, dedicated to the Lamb of God. They wait for His second coming to welcome Him in His majesty. For more than eighteen hundred years they have kept a watch on you, for Christ said that you would meet when He came again."

"And these men . . . *aarrgh*!"

Casca screamed in earnest as the cane struck him in the crotch.

"Brothers, not men. Men are a bad lot."

"Wasn't Christ a man?"

This time the cane caught him in the throat and left him gasping for breath.

"You blasphemous beast. Jesus Christ was the Son of God. No mere man."

"Well, he died like a man."

The nun's eyes widened behind her spectacles.

"You remember His death, then?"

"Yes."

Suddenly Casca did remember.

He remembered the thrust of his spear, and the storm that broke a moment later. And the Jewish prophet speaking from the cross with his last breath.

"Soldier, you are content with what you are. Then that you shall remain until we meet again. As I go now to my Father, you must one day come to me."

He remembered wiping the back of his hand across his mouth, and the one drop of the Nazarene's blood touching his tongue, burning him, sending him into a poisoned fit.

"Yes, I do remember."

"And you remember the Elder Dacort, who took your hand as punishment for profaning the holy spear."

He did remember. The Brotherhood had kept his spear, and he had felt impelled to touch it.

"It was my spear, anyway."

The rain of blows fell furiously, raising bright red weals all over Casca's body. He writhed inside the straps that restrained him.

"The spear we keep to this day. We reverence it every night."

"My spear? Here?"

The fanatic continued the whipping, panting out her words between the strokes.

"Not your spear. Our holy relic. The symbol of the watch we keep."

The violent pain was almost doing Casca good. He could feel his mind coming back to him out of the remote blankness that had succeeded the water torture, the endless hours of nothing but his own breathing and his voice counting the seconds between those relentless drops of water. By contrast, being tortured by this lunatic was almost pleasurable.

And he could feel the pain firing parts of his brain, electrifying his senses. Perhaps he could learn something, even if it meant some pain.

"What is this watch you keep?"

"We watch for you, for you will lead us to Him when He comes. Father Mulcahy is our elder. He sent me here. The Brotherhood in America told us that you were coming to the East. A brother found you in Hong Kong, but then we lost you. Then Father heard of the huge barbarian prisoner and he sent me to check. I knew you as soon as I saw you by that scar that runs from your right eye to your mouth."

Another memory came back to Casca. A whore from

Achaea who had not been amused when Casca told her, after he had had her, that he had no money.

He was brought back to the present by another whack of the cane on his balls.

"And I know it's no wound of honor, too."

Casca felt her hand on his leg.

"And here, I can feel the arrowhead that you collected in the battle for Ctesiphon on the plains of Parthia by the banks of the River Tigris. Forty-five thousand men died that day, but the curse of the Blessed Lamb kept you alive. I cannot imagine why."

The touch of a woman's hand on his thigh was pleasant.

And it stayed there. The fingers stopped probing for the arrowhead, but the old virgin left her hand on his thigh, almost caressing it. It was the first time in her life she had fondled a man's leg.

CHAPTER THIRTEEN

Several levels above where Casca lay, Baron Ying Ruochen sat sprawled on a silk-upholstered couch. There were teacups and a pot on a tray on the low table before him, and a beautiful girl squatted opposite him, waiting for his command to pour, or for whatever else he might care to command.

But the baron sat unmoving. From time to time his forehead would knit in a puzzled frown, or he would stare out of the window at the distant hills.

Of a sudden he leaped to his feet, startling the girl.

"Peace, little one," he calmed her. "Tell me, have you studied the thinking of the sage Lao-tze?"

"But of course, lord."

"And in his writings, Liang Yongming, do you remember something of a white barbarian whom he met in the far realms of Rome and who became his disciple?"

"Ah yes"—Liang smiled—"the myth of the mortal who slew the Christian demigod and became himself some sort of immortal. It is one of Lao-tze's few flights of fantasy. No doubt he invented the legend as some sort of moral lesson."

So I have always thought, the baron mused, until now. He gestured for the girl to pour his tea and sat down again.

His secretary entered and bowed respectfully.

"Baron Ying," the young man said, "Dr. Hollington Teng has arrived in Tsungkow. His messenger has just arrived, and he says that Dr. Teng is even now approaching this palace."

"Ah-ha, the very best of news. Make ready to welcome our esteemed visitor. And send our own doctor to the barbarian prisoner. Tell Poon Gong I would have Hollington Teng talk with this prisoner if there is enough of his mentality left intact to make it worthwhile."

The door to the doctor's room opened and the old nun jerked her hand away from Casca's leg. The old doctor stood in the doorway. She spoke to him in Chinese that made Casca's teeth grate.

"Good afternoon, Poon Fong, I have been giving your prisoner some spiritual guidance at the bidding of Father Mulcahy. I will go now and tell him of his condition."

She quickly left the room. The old man approached the bench. Casca saw his eyes widen as he took in the dozens of raised red welts that crisscrossed Casca's body like highlights on the network of old wound scars.

"I see that Sister Martina has been using the same form of spiritual stimulant she exercises on the boys at the Catholic school. She has great faith in the efficacy of her feather duster to inculcate spirituality."

Casca laughed heartily.

"Fortunately she is not very strong."

Poon Fong stood staring at the red weals.

"They should still be worsening, but they are fading as I watch." He ran a finger along the great scar where Casca's chest had once been opened on an Aztec pyramid.

"Baron Ying has told me that under the water treatment you told him much of mystery. I see much mystery here in these scars. This cut alone should have killed you, and I see others as bad.''

''I don't know what I told them.''

''The truth, of course.''

''But I have withstood much greater torture.''

''Perhaps. But the objective of the water treatment is not to injure the prisoner, but only to learn what he knows. It is in the nature of man to tell what he knows, and the water treatment merely removes the restraints of self-interest, loyalty, duty, and frees the tongue to relieve the mind.''

He stopped undoing the straps and stooped to stare into Casca's eyes.

''Unfortunately, when there is much resistance the eventual effect is very powerful, and the mind is left exhausted.

''Can you remember anything?''

''A little. But it doesn't seem to fit together too well.''

''Perhaps we can do something—with a little help from the gods.''

He went to the small altar that stood in the corner of the room, bowed to the brass idol, and lit two joss sticks.

''Perhaps Pao-Sheng Ta Ti, the god of healing, will assist our efforts.''

He opened a wooden box and selected a very long gold needle. He pushed it deep into Casca's abdomen. Casca looked down to see the needle penetrating deeper and deeper as the doctor twirled it. He began to feel very much at ease.

''That feels good, Doctor, but may I remind you that the problem is in my head.''

''Ah yes, I have heard of this quaint Western superstition that memory resides in the brain.''

Unconcernedly he went on twirling the long needle.

The crazy jumble of memories started once more to flash through Casca's mind.

The romping, giggling, cavorting women gave way to

one woman lying asleep, a small smile on her lips as he kissed her and slipped out of their bed.

Neda—the first woman he had really loved, and he had left her because he loved her. There were others whose faces he saw that he felt similarly for, but not too many. Mostly he saw asses and tits and felt vague stirrings of lust.

And all the men he had killed. And here and there a woman, too. There seemed to be no end to the dead.

And his own deaths. He shuddered as he relived each one. Mercifully they mostly ran together like different versions of the same experience.

He recalled enlisting in the Seventh Legion under the Emperor Augustus, then serving in the Tenth. And then he recalled that day on Golgotha when Jesus cursed him to live until he came again.

He recalled the fight with his sergeant over his whore that same night. They had killed each other, but Casca had survived. And since then he had survived countless deaths.

He had flashes of when he was a gladiator, a slave in a copper mine, a galley slave, a great chief, a warlord, a god.

He slipped into a tranquil sleep and the doctor withdrew the needle. He had done all that he could to restore the vanished memory. Sometimes it worked. Perhaps the curse that kept this strange one's body alive would also restore his mind.

CHAPTER FOURTEEN

Casca was awakened by Liang Yongming gently massaging his temples. She motioned to him to follow her and led him across a courtyard garden to a bathhouse where she handed him over to two elegant girls who conducted him to a blue stone recess in the broad white marble floor.

As Casca lowered himself into the steaming water, he ran his hands over the highly polished stone, so comfortable against his skin.

"Lapis lazuli," he wondered. "I have never seen such large pieces of this beautiful stone—must be worth a king's ransom."

After a moment the thought struck him: "And this is only a baron's guest bathroom."

The two girls washed him thoroughly, using soft cloths and a sandalwood-scented soap. Then they carefully anointed him from top to toe, deftly massaging finely perfumed oils into his every pore. All the while two pairs of lovely almond eyes watched their hands exploring this huge, white body, exchanging wondering glances as their fingers traced the patterns of the network of scars that covered the whole of Casca's body; some faded to hairlines, others still showed freshly pink.

Liang Yongming reappeared and gave Casca a richly

embroidered yellow silk robe. She conducted him to a broad chamber overlooking a courtyard, where Baron Ying sat with the recently arrived Dr. Hollington Teng.

The baron had changed his armor for a robe similar to that worn by Casca, but in the green that signified an imperial noble. Dr. Hollington Teng was dressed in the white linen suit worn by Englishmen in the tropics.

Casca bowed deeply as he entered the room, and the two Chinese bowed in acknowledgment.

"Come here, honorable barbarian," Ying said, "and sit by me. This is my esteemed friend and ally, Dr. Hollington Teng."

"How do you do?" Teng said in perfectly accented English.

"Very well, thank you," Casca replied, "and yourself?"

"I am in excellent health, thank you."

"I have told Hollington something of your history. I make no apology for the manner in which you insisted I learn it, nor for telling of it, but your secret is safe with us."

Casca bowed in acknowledgment, and the two Chinese bowed an affirmation.

"The baron and I," said Hollington Teng, "are the oldest of friends. We grew up together, and we went to England together, he to Harrow and Cambridge, myself to Eton and Oxford. I know him to be a wise and prudent man, and therefore I accept without reservation what he has told me of your history. I hope, though, that you will excuse me if I tell you that I still find it hard to believe."

"Me too." Casca laughed easily.

"Excuse me," said Ying. "Poon Fong told me that he did his best to repair your damaged mind, but that he was not sure of success as you had resisted the water treatment so mightily. Yet you seem to be in excellent spirits."

"I don't think I ever felt better," Casca smiled.

"Is that perhaps the effect of the curse you carry?"

"Perhaps, along with whatever magic Poon Fong worked with his needles."

"And your memory?"

"It seems to have returned intact."

"Good. Very good. I am pleased for you. And for us. I feel sure that you can be of service to us. We have great problems."

"Could I perhaps ask you," said Hollington Teng, "what impressions of China you have gathered on your mission?"

"The British consul's brief was that I should look for signs of unrest, and I have found it everywhere. We foreign devils are hated and feared, and not a little despised. But not more so than the Manchu emperor and especially the empress.

"I have heard much talk of the heroes of the Tsin Dynasty Revolution. Those revolutionaries are extolled as martyrs and as models."

"Exactly so," said the baron. "In the Tsin period the peasants were joined by the nobles to put an end to an unsatisfactory regime."

"Aha!" Casca exclaimed. "I think perhaps I see where you are headed."

"As you might guess from my name," said Hollington, "my family have long been involved with the British. My father went to Oxford before me. I am named for one of his masters whom he much admired and who became my godfather."

"You are a Christian then?"

"Yes—and no. I was baptized a Catholic, but I no longer follow the Church. Her ambitions for China and mine are not compatible."

"And the Raj?"

"Similarly. For a long time we cooperated with the British as we believed that we could learn much and to our mutual advantage. But in the event the advantage has been all one-sided.

"You are, of course, too young to know of the Opium War—oh, excuse me . . ."

Casca laughed easily. "Please do not concern yourself. I am not at all offended. You do me a great service in treating me as my apparent age, although you know my secret. Like anybody else, I only live one life at a time."

"I have only had the time to tell you a little of what Cas-Ca Sho has told me," said the baron. "But I can assure you that he is familiar with the opium trade."

"Indeed," Casca said frankly. "I carry some opium with me, along with silks and satins and money and other valuables for the purpose of corrupting your people in the execution of my mission."

"So has this wonderful healing agent been debased," said the doctor. "At first it was not so. China has grown and used opium for countless thousands of years. It has always been grown extensively here, and especially in Bangala and Mien, dependent states whose kings have been invested by the Chinese emperor since the time of Kublai Khan. In these territories, which you call Bengal and Burma, the climatic conditions are ideal for its cultivation.

"It was used extensively as a medicine and restorative, and also as a euphoric by those who could afford the money to buy it and the time to indulge in it. As a consequence it was so used almost exclusively by the rich and elderly, and the drug did no damage to our society.

"Portuguese traders from Goa started shipping opium, and by the early years of the eighteenth century China was importing twenty-five thousand pounds, about ten tons, a year. The Portuguese ships brought the drug to our ports as they might have carried any other cargo for which there was a demand.

"The British were growing stronger and stronger. Their small trading station on the west coast of India had grown until they held all of India, were threatening Afghanistan, and had pushed China out of Tibet.

"Every day there were many, many British ships leaving Kowloon laden with our silks and spices, exotic woods, ivory and jade carvings, porcelain and soaps and perfumes, and especially tea. The English taste for tea had become an obsession.

"These many ships arrived here empty, as we Chinese were not interested in buying cheap iron pots from Birmingham or gaudy printed cottons from Manchester or steel-nibbed pens, or any of the other products of England.

"The shipowners were unhappy about sailing so far in ballast, and the English banks were unhappy about the outflow from their stocks of precious metal for we would only accept payment for our valuable goods in ingots of silver and gold.

"Opium provided the answer to both their problems. The British Empire expanded into Bengal and Burma, acquiring at no cost both the opium crop and the labor to exploit it. Within a hundred years the opium trade multiplied a hundred times, to four million pounds, about a thousand tons, a year.

"Soon whole shiploads of the drug were arriving in Kowloon every day.

"Still there would have been little problem, but the British went about selling this drug with an intensity that we had never experienced. Very soon it was being used by young people, and by people who could not afford it, but who would commit crimes in order to be able to buy it.

"For the first time in the history of China an emperor found it necessary to intervene in the personal life of his subjects and banned the use of the drug except as a medicine. And a ban was placed on its import, as China itself produced more than what was required for strictly medicinal purposes.

"But the British were reluctant to abandon a profitable business and continued to import the drug, smuggling it into the country. They used the small offshore island Hong Kong, at that time a bleak, windswept rock, as their staging warehouse, and delivered it from there to the mainland in small boats.

"Special ships were designed and built. They carried enormous areas of sail and were tremendously fast. They brought opium from Burma to Hong Kong, and made the return voyage laden with tea for London. They were called opium clippers, then China clippers, and eventually the name was sanitized to tea clipper.

"Many fortunes were made. Tea companies and shipping companies were founded whose names are today household words. Only China was suffering.

"Then, as is in the nature of all things, the drug traffic began to flow in the other direction, too. There were British ships picking up opium in Burma and delivering it to Hong Kong where other British ships would pick it up and convey it to England, to Europe and to the United States, and in these countries the addiction began to produce the same problems as we had experienced.

"The fortunes of those involved in the trade grew to fantastic size.

"Then the English parliament passed a law prohibiting the inhalation of opium, and, as we had done, restricted its use to medicines.

"Now the British plantation owners in Burma, the tea companies, and the shipping companies had lost a major market.

"The British legation here in China informed the emperor that our legislation was offensive to Britain, and demanded that we repeal our law.

"The emperor refused, and appointed a very able imperial commissioner, Lin Tse-Hsii, to suppress the traffic.

"Lin wrote to Queen Victoria and asked her, as her own people were not permitted to inhale the drug, how could selling it be reconciled with the decrees of heaven?

"She did not do him the courtesy of a reply, and in 1839 Lin fired the British warehouses, burning the entire stock of opium.

"But more, many more ships arrived laden with the drug. The tea crop was waiting on our wharves, and in London people were waiting to buy it. Every day the tea's flavor diminished and deteriorated a little and so was worth less ôn the London market. The British ships endeavored to land their opium cargoes.

"Lin summoned all the coastal warlords, and they joined forces and blockaded the port with their junks.

"The British threatened force to break the blockade. The British parliament was divided."

The baron got to his feet and went to a bookcase. He returned with a red leather-bound volume and showed Casca the gold lettering on the spine of the book: *House of Commons, Debates, 1839*. He opened the book.

"The prime minister, the leader of the government, opposed the war. Let me read what Mr. Gladstone said to Lord Palmerston, who supported war:

" 'I will ask the noble lord a question: Does he not know that the opium smuggled into China comes exclusively from British ports? The great principles of justice are involved in this matter. You will be called upon to show cause for your present intention of making war upon the Chinese.

" 'They gave us notice to abandon the contraband traffic. When they found that we did not, they had the right to drive us from their coasts.

" 'I am not competent to say how long this war may

last, but this I can say, that a war more unjust in its origin, a war more calculated in its progress to cover this country with permanent disgrace, I do not know.' " Ying replaced the book on its shelf.

"The matter came to a head, and the British used cannon and troops to enforce our aquiescence to their demand."

"As it happened," said Hollington, "Gladstone was wrong. The British forced us to accept the opium, and seized Kowloon and Hong Kong from us into the bargain. And there was no disgrace."

"There never is for the victors," Casca said flatly.

"I wish," said Hollington, "that my father had sent me to your school where I might have learned realism, rather than to Eton where my head was filled with absurdities."

"But, perhaps," said the baron, laughing, "you may not have had the time to spare that Cas-Ca Sho has invested in his education."

All three men laughed.

"So we lost Kowloon and Hong Kong. Then, about fifteen years ago, for similar reasons, the French annexed the territory they call Cochin China and we call Vietnam. Then, claiming they disapproved of what they termed our hostile attitude to French missionaries, they declared Kampuchea what they called a 'protectorate.' Both of these territories are Chinese dependent states."

"And opium producers." Casca smiled.

"Of course. If the British had assisted us we could have expelled the French, but it suited Britain to have other colonial powers take part of our nation so long as it did not interfere with British interests.

"Then, just five years ago, the Japanese, with the connivance of the British, occupied Taiwan, which has been Chinese for centuries. And now the Japanese are building Chen-nei, a great walled city as a commercial center for

Taipei City to facilitate their exploitation of the tea crop—
our tea crop. British merchants can now buy this tea very
cheaply—for it has cost the Japanese nothing.

"And now Germany. About three years ago two German missionaries were murdered by robbers in Shantung.
Troops of all the colonial powers stormed into Kiachow
Bay and we were forced to cede the entire area to Germany for ninety-nine years. Which, as with Hong Kong,
may well be forever.

"They make an enormous and extended profit out of the
deaths of two unfortunate priests who lacked sufficient
sense to protect themselves against thieves. Hardly cricket
what?"

Casca repressed a chuckle. "I have never yet seen the
colonial game played to any rules, and certainly not cricket."

Hollington slapped his knees in exasperation. "You are
right, of course. Benjamin Jowett, master of Balliol College at Oxford, my own college, had a maxim for those
who were to join the colonial service: 'Never retract.
Never explain. Get it done and let them howl.' "

"Well," said the baron, "we are howling."

"But we must do something other than howl," said
Hollington. "The peasants are tired of howling in their
pain. Now they are howling for blood."

"When it comes to doing something," Casca interrupted, "there is another maxim to remember. It is often
chanted around the barracks of the British army: 'Whatever happens, we have got the Maxim gun—and they have
not.' "

"But we must do something. We cannot stand by and
allow our peasants to throw themselves into the hail of
lead from your Maxim guns. And we cannot be so foolish
as to join them in suicide. But—what are we to do?"

"You are asking me?" Casca asked, astonished.

"You are a man of much experience, a soldier and a diplomat. Surely you can advise us?"

Casca got to his feet and paced about the large chamber.

"I don't know just what I told you under the water treatment, and perhaps you misunderstood. I am an ordinary soldier. A sort of military bum. Certainly no diplomat. I'm a mercenary. I fight for pay. If I possessed some sort of military genius do you imagine that I would be a drill instructor in the British army?"

"But," protested the baron, "you have been a general, a chief, a king, a god."

"Surely I told you that whenever I have had that sort of promotion it has happened by chance. And then I have always fucked it up on my own account."

"But you have lived such a long time. You must have learned something."

"I'm a slow learner," Casca replied, "but if I have learned anything, it is to keep clear of fools armed with sticks and pitchforks who wish to take on empires backed by professional soldiers armed with cannon and muskets and water-cooled machine guns."

"Do you have no ideals? No principles?" exclaimed Hollington.

"Idealists wish to change the reality because it is not ideal. I have a similar problem with the ideal—it is not real. As for principles, I have always thought it would be nice to have some—but I have never found any that will stand up to gunfire. Or to swordplay, or even to an enthusiastically wielded whip."

Hollington pursed his lips and looked at the ceiling. Except for his eyes and his color, he was the very picture of the outraged English gentleman in the presence of an unprincipled cad.

Baron Ying squinted at Casca. "I do not believe you. I am sure you are a man of principle."

"And I do not believe you," Casca returned hotly. "You are rich and powerful under the Manchus. No less rich and still influential under the British. Why do you wish to ally yourself with a mob of fools bleating slogans they do not half understand?"

The baron stared evenly at Casca.

"The question is will you help us?"

Casca sat down.

"I am not British, and certainly I do not owe them anything for their lousy pay and abominable food, nor for my ridiculous uniform and the absurd discipline.

"But they have all the guns and must surely win any confrontation." He recalled that the baron had said something about rich reward. "Why should I join you?"

The baron calmly returned his gaze. "We will pay you well. And if we succeed, as we must, you will be honored and respected throughout China. And neither you, nor your descendants, will ever again want for anything."

CHAPTER FIFTEEN

Baron Ying lost no time in demonstrating to Casca that his promises were real. He summoned his secretary and dictated a letter of commission, making Casca the Hsia of Tsungkow, responsible only to himself, the baron of Chaochow, and to the emperor.

There had been no Hsia in Tsungkow for thirty-five years, the area being governed directly by the baron of Chaochow. The previous Hsia, who had also been an imperial baron, had sided with the Hakka people in their brutal conflict of 1865 with the Cantonese, losing in the Hakka defeat not only his position and his palace but also, along with many thousands of Hakka, his head.

"Hakka," Ying explained, "in our language means 'traveling family.' Three hundred years before the time when you were truly born, they were a peaceful tribe, flourishing in the fertile land between the Yellow River and the Great Wall. But their numbers increased and many moved south to the provinces of Honan and Anhwei during the Chin period, and they dwelt there for six hundred years.

"Then, during the Tsin Dynasty, around your fifth century, they were forced farther south to the mountainous reaches of Kiangsi and Fukien. Two hundred years later

119

they were pushed into the chain of mountains between Kiangsi and Kwangtung. From there they moved to the Kwangtung coast, and finally to this region and the cities of Kaying and Tsungkow and Chaochow and the villages between.

"But this traveling family does not only travel when forced to, and not only inside China. Many of the Chinese that you find in San Francisco, Bangkok, Saigon, Borneo, Singapore, Sydney are Hakka. In the Pacific islands Hakka people have become a powerful business element.

"And here, amongst us in Kwangtung Province, perhaps they have at last found a permanent home. Doubtless, in time they and we will intermarry, and eventually become one people. For myself, I must admit that I could never love a Hakka woman. Not with those big, ugly feet.

"But in everything else they are a wholly admirable people, and here they have not been subjected to any attack for thirty-five years. But then, in China's history, thirty-five years is a short time."

"A very short time." Casca laughed.

"Well, we shall see. For the present your title of Hsia will protect you from any inquiry, and I am sure you will find the tribute you collect more than adequate for your expenses.

"If it interests you, I will be pleased to hand over to you the whole government of the area and make you count of Tsungkow, an appointment which is within my power. I cannot make you baron as it is the emperor's prerogative to create imperial nobles.

"But, more importantly, what I want you to do is to use your skills and experience to prepare your troops and your city for the coming revolution. It may be necessary to put down the Boxers and the peasants; it may be necessary to join them. Perhaps we will be fighting with the emperor against the foreign devils, perhaps against both the emperor and the British. It is too early to tell.''

The baron returned to his baronial seat at Chaochow, leaving Casca in full control of Tsungkow. Casca escorted him to the city gates, then returned to his new home, the Hsia's palace.

Casca had readily agreed to take full control of the district, as he had no wish to be hamstrung by any outside authority. Nor did he intend to sit around and wait for something to happen. He intended to make his mark on the city. Fifteen hundred and more years earlier he had been an imperial baron, and now he was count of the city of Tsungkow.

Well, why not? he thought, I've been a god a couple of times.

Tian Yuanlong was waiting for him and asked him for orders.

''Who is Baron Ying's deputy in this city?'' was Casca's first question.

''The Pao, Li Peng, a good man. Baron Ying has complete trust in him.'' He smiled in quiet self-confidence. ''And I believe the baron to be a good judge of men.''

Casca smiled back. ''Yes, I do believe he is.''

''But,'' Tian went on, ''it is far from here to Chaochow Fu, and the baron is much at Chaochow.''

''So?''

''So Li Peng does not get enough of the baron's time to discuss all of our problems. Nor can I report on all of them for him, as I rarely get sufficient of his time for my own work.'' The serene smile returned. ''I am sure that you will find Li Peng as happy to serve you as Hsia as I am, Cas-Ca Sho.''

''And the city elders?''

''For the city elders your appointment as count is the

very best of news. They are, in the main, good and sincere men. Some more so than others, of course, and some who might like to be less so. But the time is always taken to ensure that any action is in the overall interests of the whole community. And, of course, no elder wishes to risk the baron's wrath by allowing self-interest to overrule his responsibility.

"But there are many matters, too, where the elders could use more of the baron's time. And there are many matters where things just have to be done without due discussion. In such cases the Hsia could act without hesitation. But who will dare take an action, perhaps against a neighbor, perhaps using the city's money? An elder, or perhaps the Pao, who is forced by circumstances to take such a responsibility, is never happy about it."

"Well, I can see I am going to have some work to do."

"Oh, estimable Hsia, I assure you there is much work to do. I would like to mention one more of Li Peng's problems."

"Please mention anytime to me any problem of the Pao's or your own."

The secretary bowed.

"Thank you, Count Cas-Ca. There are many, many small matters for which the Pao is responsible, but they are too small, or too persistent for him to be able to get any of the needed attention either from the baron or from the elders."

"Aha," said Casca, "then this is where we shall start. What is the biggest or the most persistent of these small problems?"

"The prison, sir."

"Ah, yes. Of course. And the garbage?"

A delighted smile lit Yuanlong's face. "And the garbage. Oh, Li Peng is going to very much like his new Hsia."

"Well, how do we start?"

"By now," said Tian, "all the city will know of your appointment. It only remains for them to meet you."

Tian Yuanlong organized the new Hsia's inauguration within a matter of hours.

The ringing of gongs and the beating of drums summoned the population, and soon the city square and the streets all around it were jammed with thousands of people.

Casca rode from his palace on a bay stallion with white stockings he had carefully chosen from his stables. The horse was almost identical to the one he had ridden seventeen centuries earlier when he had left the imperial palace as baron of Chung Wei. He rode at the head of a retinue of men-at-arms and knights, pikemen, archers and infantry, and the entire host of palace servants.

As soon as Casca appeared the population prostrated themselves on their faces.

Casca felt a flash of profound irritation at their exaggerated obeisance. He was about to upbraid them and tell them to get to their feet like human beings rather than cowering like dogs. But, had not he himself kowtowed? They were, after all, only giving him his due, paying respect to their new lord and master.

"I come to you as your Hsia, your count and your protector," he shouted. "Obey me and serve me well, and I will so serve you. Bring to me your problems and I will work to solve them. Come to me with your complaints and I will find you justice. But should any disobey me or be dishonest, then I will punish mightily. You may now stand."

The elite of the city had placed themselves just behind the Pao, who, with his deputies and assistants, stood between the crowd and the new Hsia. Now these gentry, the most influential clan heads, the large landlords, and the heads of the most well-to-do families, stepped forward.

The Pao stepped aside, well aware of his own relative unimportance to these men who effectively ran the city. He was relieved that Casca had shown no displeasure. It happened often enough that a newly appointed Hsia would take power in a fury of dissatisfaction, and abuse, slap, whip, or even behead the first person of authority he came upon. Which was why the elders had stayed behind him and his henchmen.

Behind the elders came servants carrying young pigs, baskets of grain, vessels of rice wine and chests of fine tea. Buddhist priests, who had also stayed safely behind the Pao's entourage, now began to beat on their gongs to frighten away any evil spirits that might try to bring misfortune to the new lord.

Casca accepted the gifts from his lofty perch and spoke briefly with each of the elders. Then he eased his horse through the small knot of elders to where the Pao stood.

Li Peng dropped to his knees and prostrated himself face down.

"Get up, Pao." Casca spoke in forceful but encouraging tones. "You are my right hand here, and I have need of your services. There is much for us to do. I believe you to be loyal and efficient. Stay so and you shall prosper greatly."

The Pao's eyes shone as he looked up at Casca, grateful for his recognition.

"I shall indeed serve you well, Lord, and indeed there is much to be done."

"Then let's get about it," Casca said. "Send these people back to their homes and their fields. Come to the palace early tomorrow."

He nodded briefly to the elders and, dismissing the crowd with a wave of his hand, turned his horse's head and rode back to his palace.

Casca's new home was enclosed by a deep ditch and a

square outer wall with an entrance gate in each side. As his entourage entered this gate about half the troops broke away and dispersed about the open area that surrounded a second wall. This open space was ornamented with beautiful trees, streams, and ponds. Stags, roebuck, and fallow deer grazed in this meadow, and on the waters there were swans, geese, duck, and other waterfowl. The streams were plentifully stocked with fish, which were restrained from escaping by copper grilles where the waters flowed out of the palace area.

The second wall had three gates to the north and three to the south, the large center gate in each group being for the exclusive use of the Hsia and nobility. As Casca and his men moved through this gate about half of his remaining troops similarly dispersed themselves about the open space surrounding a third, inner wall. This space was similarly ornamented with trees and animals. In each corner and by each gate there were buildings, which contained stores. One held all the tack needed for the horses and their armor; another, armor for the troops; another, swords, lances, bows, strings, arrows and every form of armament. One store held grain; one held wine; one was full of preserved fruits and nuts and sweetmeats; one held nothing but bedding and pillows and sheets and necessaries for the bedchambers; and one held the miscellany of materials from writing paper to cooking pots that were needed in the day-to-day life of the palace and the great number of people who lived and worked within it.

The inner wall was twenty feet high and about ten feet wide, so that it served as a terrace from which the Hsia could be seen by his people. All three walls had battlements, which were built out on corbels so that defenders atop the walls could throw down missiles, fire, hot water, or oil at attackers.

There were eight more stores inside this wall, which

held in one the Hsia's enormous wardrobe of widely varied robes; in another his personal armor; in still another everything needed for his table; and in others gold and silver bullion, precious stones, pearls, jade, coral, silver, and gold plate.

Inside the inner wall, and set well back from it, was the Hsia's palace. Its marble walls were ornamented with figures of dragons, warriors, maids, birds, and beasts, in gilt or carvings or painted. The roof was decorated in red, green, azure, and violet. The many windows were of a glass so clear that Casca at first took them to be crystal.

As he sat down in the chamber where he had first had audience with Baron Ying, Liang Yongming appeared with her tea tray to squat opposite him across the low table.

Casca was delighted to see that the baron had left this pretty young woman to attend to him.

"Most esteemed Count Cas-Ca Sho, may I tell you how happy I am to be able to serve you. Perhaps you will be so kind as to let me know your pleasure so that I may serve you as you wish." Her voice rose slightly to end in a soft giggle, which she disguised by raising one arm to hide her face behind a broad silk sleeve. She bowed deeply, touching her forehead to the floor. Then she poured fragrant tea and offered Casca a platter of dates and nuts.

Casca spent the rest of the day inspecting the palace. There were hundreds of rooms, immense stables, and impressive fortifications.

One section of the palace, separated from the rest by courtyard gardens, was set aside for the Hsia's wives and concubines. As the baron spent so little time in Tsungkow, these quarters were almost empty except for an aged eunuch and some servants and the five concubines—including the girl Liang Yongming—whom the baron had found adequate for all his needs.

Tian assured Casca that he would take immediate steps

to ensure that fifty of the handsomest young women in the city would be quickly installed in these chambers and that each day five of these would be available for attendance upon his person.

For his own private use Casca selected a small suite of rooms designed for one of the captains of the palace guard. He hastened to assure the startled Tian that for formal occasions he would continue to use the huge chambers set aside for the Hsia. But his endless lifetimes in the cramped quarters of professional soldiers had ill accustomed him to such luxury, despite the several occasions when he had enjoyed similar positions of pomp and power.

"For brief periods of time," he reminded himself aloud as he looked around at all his present splendor. "And this too shall pass . . . I wonder when."

Liang Yongming stood in the doorway of Casca's bedchamber. She explained to him that the five concubines rotated their duties on each of the baron's visits, so that, at any hour of the day or night, his every wish could be provided for. One girl supervised the kitchen and slept there, another was in charge of the bathhouse. Two girls would sleep in the outer apartment ready to run messages or otherwise do his bidding. And one girl would sleep with him in the inner chamber.

Casca looked Liang up and down, from her brilliant black hair to her exquisitely tiny slipper-clad feet.

"And whose turn is it to sleep in here?"

"Mine, Lord. Or whichever other you might prefer."

"I prefer you."

A tiny smile lit her eyes. She bowed and tripped lightly from the room to tell the others of her good fortune and dispose them about their other duties.

When she returned Casca was lying on the satin sheets of the huge bed. Liang allowed her cheongsam to fall to the floor, slipped off her slippers, and slid into the bed beside him. She lay quite still, waiting for Casca to let her know what he wanted of her.

He put one thick arm around her shoulders and she came to him, her tiny nipples turning hard as they brushed the hairs on his chest.

The first rays of the sun lit upon Casca's eyes as one of the girls from the outer apartment entered bearing a tray, which she placed on the table beside the bed. Liang quickly slipped from the bed to squat on the floor and pour the tea.

Casca watched the sky lightening. From the faint sounds reaching his chamber he could tell that people were astir throughout the palace. Good.

While he sipped his tea Casca's eyes roved over Liang's slight body, marveling at its smooth hairlessness. There was only the scant bush on the little mound between her legs. His eyes ran down her legs to her feet and he recoiled.

Alarm showed in Liang's eyes. "What is it, Lord? What displeases you?"

Casca tried to cover his revulsion. He forced his attention away from her hideously deformed feet and concentrated on the girl's tiny breasts, marvelous little mounds of muscle that rose only slightly above the curve of her chest.

He moved his attention to her lovely eyes.

"You please me greatly, little one. I merely had an old, unpleasant thought," he lied. "An ugly old memory flashed into my mind. But it is gone now."

Fortunately it would not cross Liang's mind that her feet were involved. Had not the baron told her often that she had the most beautiful feet he had ever seen? And she knew that the baron had known countless women. Casca put out his arm and she curled herself into it. Looking into her eyes, he smiled tenderly, thinking that it would not be too hard to keep his eyes above her knees.

Liang happily nipped his ear with her small, white teeth. As she nibbled at his earlobe Casca took the opportunity to study her feet while she could not see his face.

Oh, my God. I had quite forgotten how horrible this absurdity can be. Casca remembered vividly his first experience of the only institutionalized perversion that he had found in the land of Chin.

Baby Chinese girls had their feet bound soon after birth, and their feet stayed about the same size and appeared exquisitely tiny in shoes. But when seen naked the feet had grown to a monstrous shape, a great curving instep, the span of a normal foot, that bridged the space of barely three inches from heel to toe.

Fei Jiyan, his whore in Hong Kong, had been born in the street and orphaned early so that her feet had never been bound, perhaps one of the reasons she was condemned to whoredom in the cheapest of back-street shacks.

And Ju Songzhen, whom he had enjoyed in Shou-Chang, was of the Hakka people, who despised and abhorred the custom of foot binding. The Hakka were always on the move, and their women were proud of their ability to walk long distances carrying huge loads, and to fight beside their men when need be.

In the best and most settled and prosperous times, the Hakka women worked beside their men in the fields. Where else would a woman want to be? The children worked, too. Where else could they want to be? The whole family would take turns to walk behind the plow—and to pull it if they were too poor to own an ox. They were a barefoot people who walked everywhere, planted from cane baskets, gathered their crops by hand, winnowed the chaff in the wind, drew their water from a pool, and made bricks with mud and straw.

And when their men were fighting, which was much of the time, or working overseas, these women did all of the heavy work, and they developed strong, beautiful feet.

Liang's feet, Casca thought, were truly hideous.

The binding had ensured that her toes were only a few inches from her heels. But the foot had grown anyway, rising in a great ugly lump of instep that curved in an arch from the heel to the toes. The effect was entirely horrible.

CHAPTER SIXTEEN

Casca was still eating his breakfast of rice soup when Tian Yuanlong came into the room to ask for orders and to tell him that the Pao, Li Peng, was also waiting to see him.

Over cups of steaming tea the three men discussed the most pressing problems of the city, especially the unsanitary condition of the streets. Casca ordered that every man in the village who lacked land or employment be put to work immediately to clean up the streets and to dig a large excavation on some wasteland beyond the city walls where all of the city's rubbish would be buried.

"But, who will pay these men for so much work?" Tian asked.

"For the moment I will," Casca replied without hesitation. "Later, when an economical routine has been established, I shall set a tax to be levied upon all those who own property or do business within the city walls."

The Pao was mightily pleased at this news. All his efforts toward cleaning the streets had been frustrated by lack of money and the persistent refusal of the city elders to tax themselves for the purpose.

He assured Casca that the streets would be clean by that very evening, and that all of the garbage would be buried by the next day. He hurried away to get the work started.

Casca called for the captain of the palace guard, liked him at a glance, and promoted him to colonel of the city. Huang Chu accompanied Casca on a tour of the palace defenses and Casca specified the changes that he wanted made. When they came back to the audience chamber the Pao was waiting for more orders, having instructed his deputies to start cleaning up the city.

Casca rode with him to the prison where he had all the prisoners paraded. There were not many of them. Chinese society depended upon family and social pressures to keep people within the law, and most serious infractions were punished with either death or mutilation. The prisons usually held only those awaiting trial, or being otherwise detained. Long-term imprisonment was not used as a punishment.

The turnkey told him that some of the present prisoners were rapists, murderers, or thieves, but that most of the others had been imprisoned for evading taxes, resisting orders of the emperor, or for indulging in some form of revolutionary activity. However, in the wake of the Hakka civil war, the execution of the previous Hsia, and the subsequent death from old age of his scribe, some of the records had been lost while others were illegible; and with the older prisoners it was now impossible to tell which prisoner had been sentenced for what crime.

Seven of the prisoners were in pathetic condition, their bodies atrophied and distorted from long confinement. Another three had festering hands, the wrists rubbed through to the bone by their heavy iron manacles.

Casca spoke briefly to Li Peng and then addressed the prisoners.

"Hear me. I am Count Cas-Ca Sho, Hsia of this county. I intend to rule justly, decently, and, I trust, wisely."

From the corner of his eye he saw that the orders he had

given Li Peng were already being carried out. He motioned to Peng, and the seven near-dead and the men with the festering arms were picked up bodily and carried to where ten swordsmen stood waiting.

At a nod from Casca the long, curved swords flashed in the sun and seven heads and three arms fell to the ground, followed by all ten bodies. The men who had lost their arms were already unconscious when their bleeding stumps were cauterized with a flaming torch.

Casca cleared his throat. "As you see, my justice is swift and severe. Each of you will now receive a bath, some clean clothes, and enough money to keep you for one week. Those of you who have not found employment at the end of the week shall report to the Pao and he will put you to work cleaning the city.

"Those of you who repeat your past mistakes and come back here shall be treated as these ten have been."

A murmur of relief ran through the crowd of prisoners and Casca grinned to himself. Maybe not the wisdom of Solomon, but it seems to have served the purpose.

He gestured dismissal and the prisoners were led away to be bathed and fed and outfitted and then paid off as he had promised. Now it was time for him to prepare to meet the baron. He had been informed of his coming this very night and he was bringing guests of import with him.

Casca and Baron Ying were seated at a low table in Casca's palace studying maps of Kwangtung Province when Tian Yuanlong entered the room to announce the arrival of visitors.

Three Chinese men entered the chamber, all dressed in double-breasted European suits with shirts and ties. A middle-aged man led the way; the two younger men who followed him wore their hair cut short. They were the first two Chinese Casca had ever seen without pigtails.

They were brought up short by the sight of Ying in his baronial robes talking to a foreign devil who was also wearing the robes of a Chinese of high rank.

In some confusion, the three visitors bowed, and Ying and Casca bowed in greeting.

"Cas-Ca Sho," said the baron, "allow me to introduce some of the very best and most dedicated of our allies. This is Mr. Song, whose business is selling the Bible."

The middle-aged Chinese bowed.

"Mr. Song is estimated to be the richest man in the world, and he is making quite a portion of his immense fortune available to the movement. And this is Dr. Sun Yat-sen, who has studied in Hong Kong."

The ascetic-looking Sun bowed.

"And this is David Sen-yung, who has just returned from Hong Kong where he has been studying to become a teacher.

"Gentlemen, I would like you to meet the honorable Count Cas-Ca Sho, a barbarian whom I very much respect and who has joined cause with us."

Each of the Chinese advanced in turn and shook hands, Sen-yung saying in confident but badly spoken English: "I am very pleased to meet you, honorable barbarian." But Casca saw that his eyes remained wary toward him.

Casca clapped his hands and Liang Yongming appeared with the tea tray and squatted at the table by the five men. As she poured tea and handed around small cakes the baron suddenly turned to Casca.

"What do you know of the Marquis of Queensberry?"

"Nothing good," Casca mumbled through a mouthful of delicious rice cake.

David Sen-yung sat bolt upright, his eyes wide in amazement. Ying, too, stared at Casca. Sun smiled, while Mr. Song merely looked at Casca carefully.

Sen-yung opened his mouth to protest, then stopped and

looked to the baron. Ying gestured his approval and the young Chinese spoke with considerable force.

"Surely you cannot know anything but good of the father of the noble art of self-defense?"

'The dubious art of the closed fist?'' Casca shrugged. "It was practiced in ancient Rome, and before that in Greece. They used weighted gloves so that most boxers died in the ring, whereas with Queensberry's rules they survive for many fights, and still die from the blows they take. But they die outside the ring, and so it is held more respectable.

"Queensberry has merely codified it so that gentlemen, and gentlewomen, can more conveniently wager upon the outcome of two dumb beasts belaboring each other toward unconsciousness and eventual stupidity and death.

"And, for self-defense, the closed fist is but a clumsy thing alongside K'ung Fu-tzu's art of the open hand."

Sun Yat-sen looked in confusion from Casca to Ying and back to Casca.

"But," he protested, "Confucius is an archaic thinker. As is the way of the open hand an outdated system of self-defense. We are upon the threshold of the twentieth century. It is time to discard all this time-worn nonsense that keeps us in backwardness."

Sen-yung spoke: "Would you believe me, sir, that there are people in my country who, when ill, prefer to submit to the superstitious practice of acupuncture needles rather than utilize the sophisticated medicines of men of modern knowledge such as Dr. Sun Yat-sen?"

Casca smiled. "I believe I am one."

Sen-yung's mouth dropped open and the baron, laughing, hastened to intervene.

"David is the very prototype of the new Chinese man. He is obsessed with such ideas as the telegraph and flying balloons. He dreams of flying machines. Any machines, eh David?"

"So long as those machines are controlled by Chinese," Sen-yung responded primly.

"Indeed. David is an ardent revolutionary. He is a member of a sect which is at the core of the movement. They espouse everything that is modern or from the West—"

"Other than domination by the West," interposed Sen-yung.

"Exactly. His sect practices boxing as a rite."

Great fucking balls of Mars! Casca exploded inwardly. What the fuck have I got myself into?

"It is time," said the baron, "for us to put all our cards on the table, as you English say." He smiled to Casca, letting him know that his true story was not to be one of the cards.

"We are running very short of time. And we do not have very many choices. The peasants will erupt any day. If we do not join them they will probably lose, and the power of the British and the other colonial powers will be increased."

"China is in the position of a sub-colony," Sun Yat-sen interposed. "A country not simply oppressed or protected by one state, but subject to the encroachments of all the great powers combined."

"Your military sage, Sun Tzu, would suggest that you find a way to divide that combination," Casca declared.

Yat-sen looked at him in puzzlement. "You are a very curious Englishman, Count Cas-Ca. You deride Queensberry and extol Chinese thinkers."

Casca shrugged. "Just observation of what works best, Doctor."

"It is surely clear"—Yat-sen seemed to be making an effort to be patient—"that your Lord Palmerston and

General Chinese Gordon are better military strategists than Sun Tzu?''

"I doubt that," Casca replied easily. "I would recommend that you study Sun Tzu's *The Art of War*."

"War is not my business," Sun Yat-sen replied. "I am a philosopher. When it comes to war, that is the province of men such as Baron Ying, and, I presume, yourself. I am only concerned with moving my country toward revolutionary change."

"Perhaps"—Mr. Song spoke for the first time—"honorable Cas-Ca Sho has a point. Let us consider this another time."

The baron took over the discussion again.

"We know from our experiences with the Opium War and the Taiping Rebellion, that a defeat will be followed by disastrous reprisals and the exaction of even more cessions of territory and sovereignty.

"On the other hand, if the peasants should win without our assistance, they may succeed in pushing the colonial powers into the China Sea, but, I fear, they will throw with them all that is good in our present system. All that we have learned over thousands of years about governing ourselves."

"I have heard from Wong Sam Ark," said Mr. Song.

"Aha." The baron sounded pleased. "What says the Master?"

"Wong," Mr. Song explained for Casca's benefit, "is Supreme Grand Master of the Worldwide Order of Chinese Freemasons." To Ying he added: "He counsels that we wait."

"Wait?" The baron was on his feet, slapping his hands in impatience. "Wait for what?"

"For developments." Song shrugged.

Over the succeeding weeks Casca was to get to know several more of the leaders of the odd assortment of revolutionaries who were plotting to free China from the colonial yoke: Nominal Christians like Mr. Song, Freemasons, Socialists, Warlords, and peasants. He developed a particular fondness for the cranks who proudly referred to themselves as Boxers. The more he saw of them, the better Casca liked these intense young men, but the less he understood them.

Their primary objective was the expulsion from China of all Europeans; and of every vestige of European influence except for machines, cannon, muskets, locomotives, surgery, dentistry, optometry, motor cars, hot air balloons, the telephone, sewing machines, fountain pens, the English language, the Bible; and the thinking of Thomas Paine, Karl Marx, and, especially, the Marquis of Queensberry.

They also wanted to scrap the teachings of K'ung Fu-tzu and Lao-tze, and the medical science that dated back to the time of Huang Ti, the Yellow Emperor, who had lived four thousand years before Casca was born.

CHAPTER SEVENTEEN

The Year of the Boar was coming to a close, to usher in the Year of the Rat, the first year in each cycle of twelve years. In the Western calendar the new year would also signal the start of a new century.

In London there was dignified but frantic diplomatic activity as the ambassadors of Germany, Holland, Portugal, the United States, Japan, Russia, and France sought to dissuade the British government from declaring Queen Victoria empress of China.

Reports of these maneuverings came back to China and prompted Mr. Song to make another journey to Tsungkow, before the new year, this time to consult with Casca.

"There is only one colonial power who has not exacted cession of territory," Casca pointed out, 'and that is the United States. Why don't you go to Washington and talk to them?"

Mr. Song smiled bitterly. "It is true that America has not seized any of our territory, but under what England's Lord Palmerston derided as the Me Too policy, they demand in each ceded territory the same privileges as the foreign power who holds the territory.

"Worse yet, some of the colonial powers have able and incorruptible administrators and soldiers whom we deal with. Even the worst of them have some awareness of our position and of the limits to exploitation. With America we must deal with businessmen. And, as I am one myself, I can tell you there is no end to the rapaciousness of a businessman.''

Casca nodded. ''True. Even looting soldiers can be controlled to some extent, but there is no controlling a greedy businessman.''

''Besides''—Song shook his head—''I am a true Chinese and I will never leave China. When I was a little boy pulling a ricksha, I saw the great English general Chinese Gordon. He walked into battle with nothing to defend him but the Bible under his arm. I was converted on the spot to the power of the Bible.''

''You are a Christian then?''

''Certainly not. But I saw that there were going to be many Bibles sold in China, so I started selling them. Perhaps only one Chinese in ten thousand buys a Bible, but that is a lot of Bibles. Nor are my three daughters Christians. I have great ambitions for them as I have not been blessed with sons.''

''If you wish me to give you advice,'' Casca said, ''you should be frank with me about your ambitions.''

Song shrugged. ''Our society is divided into the Shih, the educated scholars; Nung, the farmers; Kung, handicraft workers; and at the bottom of the scale, Shang, the merchants.

''It is no disgrace for me that I was once a ricksha coolie. But while the Shih may retire from their studies and professions to become public leaders, the Shang may not. I know myself to be an intelligent man, and I can afford to be honest on behalf of my country, but as a merchant I am not welcome in the halls of power.''

''Then you should certainly go to the United States. There, merchants are welcome in places of power.''

"So I have heard. Perhaps I shall send Sun Yat-sen to America. If his revolution succeeds I will marry my daughter Song Mai Ling to him. In this way I will achieve a say in the affairs of my country."

"And the other two daughters?" Casca queried.

Again the Chinese shrugged. "I will marry them to his most promising rivals."

After the departure of Song, Casca was left to celebrate the New Year and the start of the twentieth century with a splendid dinner, some bottles of rice wine, and the enjoyment of all five of his duty concubines.

He had managed, while avoiding insult, to persuade Tian Yuanlong to select half of his fifty wives from the Hakka people, claiming that, as they made up about half of the population, their daughters should share the honor of sleeping with the Hsia and catering to his every need and whim.

He did not mention that the attraction for him was their unbound feet. But despite her deformed feet, Liang Yongming remained his favorite and shared his bed more often than all the others.

Casca's five million subjects in the city and county didn't commence their New Year festivities until two weeks later, the sixteenth of January on the European calendar.

Then the merchants balanced their books, giving thanks to the gods for their gift of a prosperous year and praying for another one. All debts were paid so that the new year might start in perfect communion with other merchants. In households knives and scissors were hidden so that none might cut the continuity of luck for the future.

In the palace Liang Yongming sealed the lips of the kitchen god, Tsou Shen, with a malt jelly so that he would only say sweet things on his visit to the heavens at this time. She also gave him rice wine to make him drunk so that his reports would be lax and erroneous. And she provided him liberally with paper money for his journey.

"I could use a good report with the gods," Casca said as he added a whole English pound to the pile. "Let's see what the Chinese gods in the other world think of English money. The whole of this world is crazy about it."

Tsou Shen and the money disappeared, and while the idol was away the whole of the palace was thoroughly cleaned, every member of the household, including Casca, Tian Yuanlong, the doctor Poon Fong, and Huang Chu, now colonel of the city, helping to clean, rearrange, and paint.

A new idol appeared in the oven and a banquet celebrated his return. All the children in the palace got special attention, new clothes, and some money.

The youngest members of the palace guard formed a dragon, one of them carrying the great papier-mâché head, and eighteen others running under the red, gold, and green tail as, accompanied by fireworks, the dragon visited every doorway and room in the palace.

For a whole month the celebration went on. Each ward of the city, and each town and village in the county, had its own dragon, and night after night these dragons chased away the evil spirits that might have taken up residence during the past year. The dragons scared them into the open where fireworks and rockets terrified them back to their own evil realms.

On the fifteenth of February on the English calendar the festivities for the Festival of Lanterns ended. Thousands of lamps were carried through the streets and houses and in and out of every room and cupboard to show the good spirits that no evil spirits remained in places or people, and to light the way so that these good spirits might find themselves comfortable abodes with the families for the forthcoming year.

The festival ended with a prodigious meal, and all families went quietly and early to bed. By midnight the city was silent, except for the European quarter, where the celebration went on all night, European-style, with champagne and whiskey and cigars.

On the sixteenth, all hell broke loose.

At the first explosion, just before dawn, Liang Yongming leaped from Casca's bed and ran to the window. Casca laughed heartily as she cowered behind the curtain, trembling as she stared out at the palace grounds.

"What happens? What happens?" she moaned.

The door burst open and the two concubines from the outer chamber rushed in looking similarly terrified. Eyes wide in their heads, they fluttered to the window in frightened bewilderment.

Casca chuckled delightedly at the performance they were putting on for his benefit, pretending fright at the fireworks, which certainly were the loudest and most prolonged of the month's festivities.

But when Huang Chu, the colonel of the city, appeared in the doorway, Casca hurtled from his bed, cursing himself for not registering alarm earlier.

Behind Huang Chu were half a dozen men carrying the many pieces of his armor, and they started placing these on Casca's body as Huang Chu explained to him that the peasants were attacking the foreign legations, mission churches and schools, and foreign-owned warehouses and businesses.

All Chinese would know that there would be no fireworks after the Festival of the Lanterns, which signified that all evil spirits had been frightened away. But the rebels had banked on the foreign devils' ignorance, hoping that they would take the explosions for harmless celebration.

The Boxers had taken matters into their own hands

without waiting for the nobles, the rich merchants, or the Freemasons to come to a decision.

"And damned good thinking too," Casca muttered as the armorers linked together the separate pieces that protected his arms, shoulders, armpits, and abdomen. All were made of canvas sewn with iron plates that had been elaborately lacquered to prevent rusting, the plates covered on the outside with blue silk and red velvet. The shoulder pieces had a golden dragon embroidered on each. The separate pieces were covered by a vest of the same material, and apronlike pieces covered the legs.

Casca thrust his feet into the boots of black silk with heavy cord soles as one of the men looped over his shoulders the straps for an armored bow case of fringed velvet, and the quiver for the five ceremonial arrows of yellow willow with spiral goose feathers. Taking from one of the armorers a sharkskin scabbard, he drew from it a straight, double-edged sword with a grooved blade almost a yard long, the hilt of carved white jade. He was already walking quickly from the chamber as the other armorer placed on his head a helmet of steel with gilded mounts set with ruby, coral, malachite, and turquoise. Casca added the face mask he had taken from the dead Hu Wei and stuck the Webley in his belt. Lastly he snatched up his armored gloves. As he walked through the doorway a smiling Huang Chu handed him a mace.

Casca thanked him and hefted the leather-wound iron handle. The pear-shaped brass head had a Chinese character repeated around it in relief. Casca chuckled and bowed to Huang as he recognized "sho"—long life.

From the top of the palace wall Casca could see fires burning throughout the European quarter. In the city itself there were other fires burning in mission churches, monasteries, and schools. And the whole of the waterfront and warehouse district appeared to be in flames.

"Shit," Casca breathed. "They're not fucking about, are they?"

Inwardly he fumed. He should have known. If there were to be an uprising it had to be soon or never. He should have seen that and insisted that Baron Ying and his supporters and allies come to the necessary decisions and make appropriate preparations. Had he thought more about it he should have been able to predict that this very morning would be the time for the uprising to start.

As it was, the baron was still surveying the route for the stringing of a telegraph wire from Chaochow to Tsungkow, when they might have already completed it by simply following either the road or the river.

Well, at least the things that were within Casca's own domain had been seen to. Baron Ying had charged him with the defense of the city and the palace, and these defenses and the troops were in the best possible condition.

So now, the rebellion was here. But who was fighting whom? And what side was Casca on?

The only man who could tell him was two days away downriver, and, no doubt, just as confused and busy with a similar situation.

Which meant that Casca had to make his own decisions. Fine.

Under the Treaty of Tientsin, every one of the dozens of fires he could see was the direct responsibility of the emperor and himself as the emperor's representative.

So, to comply with the terms of the treaty, he should immediately devote his entire resources to extinguishing the fires, finding and punishing the perpetrators, and crushing the incipient rebellion.

In the first place, for all Casca knew, Baron Ying and his allied nobles, and perhaps even the emperor, had joined the rebels. In the second place, extinguishing the fires was clearly impossible.

In the third place, he didn't want to. His own sympathies were squarely with the rebels.

If the colonial powers were to win, they would certainly unleash the same sort of reprisals as had followed the collapse of the Taiping Rebellion, shelling cities, laying waste to the countryside, executing ringleaders and responsible nobles, exacting the cession of more territory and power.

Casca had no choice. The Boxers must win.

He turned to Huang Chu. "Ready the troops. We're going to sack the British legation."

"Yes, sir." Huang saluted briskly and signaled to his waiting captains. Their pleased smiles removed the last of Casca's doubts.

CHAPTER EIGHTEEN

Casca had no sooner issued the order than he began to kick himself for his own negligence. He scarcely even knew where to find the British Legation, much less how to attack it. He had naturally made a point of staying well away from it. To be discovered by the British could only result in the hanging that he had been promised in Hong Kong.

From the ramparts of the outer wall of his palace, Casca and Huang Chu surveyed the burning city. It wasn't hard to pick out the European quarter. The lightening sky was not as bright as the fires that blazed in all of the foreign legations.

"Do you know anything of the defenses of this British legation?" Casca asked Huang.

"Oh yes," his colonel replied, and Casca breathed a sigh of relief—which was followed by a sharp intake of breath as Huang continued, "It's virtually impregnable."

"Great."

Casca turned from the raging conflagration to scan the palace defenses.

He was quickly satisfied. He had been much impressed at first sight with the defensive layout of the palace, and was confident in the improvements he had ordered. If worse came to worst, and the palace came under attack, he was confident he could hold it against any force that was likely to come against it, short of the entire British army.

And the city walls were similarly secure against attack from the outside. But from inside the city there was the certain threat of a counterattack from the foreign legations. Of these, only the British had forces of any significant size. Hence a preemptive strike against this legation made good military sense.

But, from what Huang said, the British had already taken this into account and so had taken the appropriate measures to protect their legation.

Casca didn't have to think too hard to envisage some of these measures: a fortress as near to impregnable as stone and steel could make; a contingent of well-trained, highly disciplined, and well-armed troops; stores and supplies and ammunition sufficient to withstand a siege for almost forever—and lots of Martini Henry and Lee Enfield rifles with dumdum bullets, water-cooled machine guns, and assorted cannon. And all of this enclosed in a bastion of earthworks faced with stone.

And Casca's troops would be attacking this fort with bows and arrows, lances, and swords.

"Hmmm."

And the initiative had been taken out of his hands,

The Boxers were already leading thousands of peasants in suicidal attacks on all the foreign legations, clambering up the outer walls on bamboo ladders and ropes hung from crude iron hooks.

In the near distance Casca could see the Chinese attackers already falling back from the walls of the British legation, leaving bodies lying at the foot of the walls. The firing from the half-awake and hungover defending troops was sporadic, but effective enough against people armed with billhooks and scythes, hoes and kitchen knives.

The only redeeming feature that Casca could see was that there was a fierce fire burning inside the legation, as there was in almost every building in the foreign quarter.

"These fires were started by Chinese servants inside the legations?" he asked Huang. The colonel nodded.

Casca didn't bother asking about the fate of these servants. By now all the foreign-devil officers would be well awake, their hangovers only serving to worsen their tempers. Few of the servants who had set the fires would still be alive.

A beautiful opportunity had been wasted. The precious element of surprise had been squandered.

But, fortunately, the morning breeze was fanning the fires, and inside the legations the defenders would have to use more and more men to try to quench the flames, leaving less to defend the walls.

The time to attack was now. But how?

Already Casca's troops—infantry, archers, pikemen, and cavalry—were amassed by all the palace gates, waiting only for the word to pour out into the city.

Runners had carried the message to the several troop stations throughout the city and at the city gates, and these troops, too, were now waiting for the order to attack the detested foreign devils. All told, something like thirty thousand warriors were waiting on Casca's order to attack perhaps three hundred British soldiers.

Still Casca hesitated.

Besides his regular troops there were the peasants led by the Boxers, and these probably numbered another thirty thousand, perhaps many more.

Still Casca hesitated.

With good reason. The Boxers and their peasants were already in tragic disorder. Here and there they were hurling themselves at the walls of one or another of the legations, most of them cut down by rifle fire before they even reached the earthworks. The ground around the walls was littered with corpses, and the shrieks of the dying carried to Casca on the palace walls.

The narrow, twisting streets were jammed with tens of thousands of shouting Chinese, the ones at the rear vigorously shouting slogans and pushing forward, those at the front bleeding and screaming, holding their wounds as they sought escape from the withering hail of lead from the legation walls, which increased in force and effectiveness by the minute.

The entire foreign quarter was protected from any attack by Casca's troops by the mass of peasants milling uselessly in the streets.

From all quarters the city's captains were looking up to where Casca and Huang stood on the palace wall. Beside them the signal archers waited expectantly, their great eight-foot bows, the largest Casca had ever seen, in their hands; ming-tis, the whistling arrows, ranged along the parapet ready to carry Casca's message to the thousands of waiting warriors.

Casca glanced along the line of ming-tis. The smallest of them was four feet long with a huge head of lacquered wood the size of an apple pierced through with holes so that it emitted a piercing shriek as it flew. Other arrows had heads of bone or of iron and, with their cunningly pierced holes and their sharp, heavy points, could be relied upon to deliver their message effectively both to the attacking troops who heard them, and to the unfortunate defenders who received them.

Casca had familiarized himself with the signaling system, and had come to admire its ingenuity. Each arrow made a distinctive sound, carrying its own unique message to the troops who heard it as it winged its way to the enemy.

But just now he could see no way to use the system.

What he needed was a signal that would tell the rioting peasants and their fanatic leaders to go home and leave the fighting to those who knew something about it.

Unfortunately, the whistling signal arrows were part of the old China, which was totally despised by the Boxers who were leading the rioting peasants. If by some chance they should understand an arrow's message, they would certainly ignore it, no matter how sensible. On the other hand, they would slavishly follow any message they might receive through some modern agency such as the telegraph. But there wasn't any telegraph—other than that operated by the British.

At the thought Casca turned to Huang. "Get some men through to the telegraph lines. Cut the wires. Fell the poles. Set fire to them, anything. Break the communication any way you can."

He knew it was already too late, that already the wires had carried news of the uprising to the British authorities in Swatow, perhaps to Hong Kong, very likely even to London.

The Morse telegraph girdled the earth. How far could a whistling arrow hope to reach?

He asked the archer next to him and was astonished when the man casually pointed to the French legation almost half a mile away.

The British legation was much closer, perhaps only three hundred yards. A rare enough bow shot. But when he pointed to it the archers nodded confidently.

It was now full daylight, and on the bastion of the legation a red-coated British officer was in full view, the morning sun glinting on the splendid gold braid on his helmet and epaulets as he directed the fire of his men.

Casca pointed him out to one of the archers.

He selected a reed arrow with a simple pointed iron cap and fitted the horn nock to his bowstring. Casca heard the slap of the bowstring against the bamboo bracer, which protected the archer's left wrist, and in the same instant saw the officer tumble backward from the wall.

"Well," Casca mused, "perhaps all is not lost."

He quickly ordered Huang to put all of his archers into action immediately, stressing that they should shoot from the greatest possible range, and stay under cover as much as possible.

A second later three giant whistling arrows flew toward the legation walls, and in another second they were followed by a hail of perhaps a thousand arrows that swept the walls clear of defenders.

Screaming and shouting exultantly, hundreds of peasants clambered up the ladders and threw new ropes over the walls.

Few of them even made it to the top of the wall, as new defenders appeared and cut them down with rifle shots or bayonet thrusts.

But many redcoats died, and the Chinese dead were quickly replaced from behind. The corpses piled up at the foot of the legation walls, but each corpse had cost the British a bullet.

"And I've got more Chinese than they've got bullets," Casca muttered, but cursed that he could not order a retirement of the peasants, conserving some of their lives, and clearing some space for an attack by his warriors.

A new sound struck Casca's ears, and the chatter of machine guns was accompanied by a horrible cacophony of screams and shrieks and groans as the withering fire hosed the rioters into bloody heaps.

Still, as fast as the Chinese fell, others pressed from behind to take their place.

Casca grimaced at the slaughter, but reckoned the cost in bullets to his own advantage.

Another wave of arrows silenced the machine guns, and

a few peasants made it onto the wall where they fought hand to hand with the British soldiers.

Uselessly.

They were all dead within moments, and the deadly chatter started again.

Soon the mass of the peasants would realize what was happening and, Casca reasoned, they would break and run, leaving the streets free for his troops. He told Huang Chu to start the attack as soon as this happened, and Huang Chu ran to where an ostler waited by the gate with his horse.

The moment came, and the tide of shouting Chinese turned. Those at the rear who did not realize the retreat was occurring still tried to press forward but were trampled by the terrified ones fleeing in horror. They had seen close up the effects of the hollow-nosed ammunition as it plowed through the bodies in front of them, exiting through holes the size of a man's fist, spraying those behind with buckets of blood and chunks of hot dripping flesh.

But Casca's archers, still firing from cover at long range, continued to whittle away the gunners, and when the guns were quieted for a moment the first of Huang's infantry rushed the legation walls.

The sudden arrival of disciplined warriors was a bad shock to the defending soldiers, who quickly found they had a real fight on their hands.

The carnage amongst Casca's troops was enormous, but here and there where the defense faltered one of Casca's men would gain the top of the wall, in many cases because a rifle had jammed, or the defender had run out of ammunition. Empty rifles and bayonets were poor defense against swords and the small bows and arrows carried by the Chinese infantry.

The machine-gunners were special targets, and they were butchered mercilessly as they strove to turn their clumsy weapons from aiming at the street to fire along the top of their own wall. And, when they did succeed, they shot as many of their own men in their frantic attempt as they did attackers.

Casca raced around the walls of the legation, his horse slipping and sliding in puddles of blood, leaping over the dead and dying, or pounding them into the cobblestones with its hooves.

In one street he came upon David Sen-yung, haranguing the fleeing peasants, exhorting them to return to the walls and certain death. Casca grabbed him around the waist and hoisted him onto his horse, turning to head back to the palace gates.

Inside the portal he lowered Sen-yung to the ground.

As the young Boxer opened his mouth to speak, Casca cuffed him unceremoniously with the back of his armored glove, knocking him to the ground.

"Kowtow," he shouted, as the dazed rebel managed to get to his hands and knees and obediently bowed his head to the ground.

"Are you all right?" Casca asked, carefully keeping the concern out of his voice.

"Yes, I've been lucky—or unlucky."

"Damned fucking lucky, you young fool. Luckier than you deserve, and don't you mistake it. Now get up off the ground and get yourself a decent weapon and get your ass back out there.

"Regroup all the men you can behind buildings the enemy's guns can't reach. Order any other Boxers, in my name, to do the same in dispersed areas of the city.

"And wait for fucking orders—do you know the whistle code?"

"Of course."

''The gods are smiling.''

He grabbed the bemused David by the arm and squeezed it, then wheeled his mount and raced back out through the gate.

CHAPTER NINETEEN

Huang Chu met him in the street outside the legation, where he was directing the action below the one wall that his troops had taken. Hundreds of men were now pouring up the ladders. The Chinese had fought their way to one corner and were almost to the other.

They advanced on the British riflemen, the Chinese falling in turn as their bodies soaked up the bullets until each rifleman found his five-round magazine empty and had to try to wield his clumsy nine-pound rifle and bayonet against the two or three or four or five swords facing him on the wall.

And the Chinese soldiers behind these swordsmen sheathed their swords and drew the small bows they carried behind their backs. Each man's quiver carried only a handful of light arrows, but at the close range they were soon accounting for riflemen faster than the British could kill the swordsmen.

A British bugle sounded retreat, and in the street Casca heard it and swung around to Huang.

"Call everybody back. Now. Retreat. Get the men off the walls."

Huang looked surprised and confused, but signaled his archers, and the whistling arrows soared almost vertically,

shrilling their message, and howling it again as they plum-
meted down to thud into the ground inside the legation.

But even the best-trained troops are easier to recall when
they are losing than when they are tasting victory. The
order was obeyed, but tardily. Every Chinese who was
within arm's reach or bow shot of a foreign devil hesitated
just long enough to help him along the way to meet his
ancestors.

"Too fucking late," Casca cursed, as he heard the
machine guns open up from within the legation. Half a
dozen British crews were now operating guns from the
legation grounds, spraying the walls with death, and ruthlessly wiping out any of their own men who had been
tardy to answer the retreat.

Hundreds of Chinese were falling into the streets. Every
fifth bullet was hollow-nosed, and expanded on impact to
tear off an arm or a leg, or to blow a hole through a man's
gut that would accommodate a football.

The upward tilt of the guns sent great chunks of bleeding meat and tripe flying skyward. The streets were spattered with a rain of blood and meat and guts and shit and
spent lead.

Countless, perhaps more than a thousand, Chinese were
dead, and another thousand or so were dying in moaning
agony all around the legation bastion.

As near as Casca could estimate the British had lost
something like thirty men and were now back in control of
the whole of the legation territory.

The best that Casca could hope for was that his archers
might be able to keep the British from remounting their
machine guns atop the walls.

Stalemate. Casca fumed.

With some artillery he might have blown some holes in
the walls, but the Chinese had no cannon.

But they did have rockets. Casca consulted with Huang,

some signal arrows flew, and within a few seconds fiery trails were howling from the palace.

The first few rockets went wild, landing amongst Casca's own troops, blowing great bleeding spaces in their ranks; but the gunners in the palace quickly adjusted their aim, and soon a rain of fire was falling inside the legation.

Huang Chu also brought up some companies of men armed with agny astras, long bamboo tubes that discharged fire-tipped darts. He dispersed these all around the legation and they poured their fire over the walls. They could accomplish little damage, but they did keep a lot of the British troops busy putting out the fires that they started.

The main fire was now being brought under control, and soon the British would be able to strike back.

The thought had scarcely touched Casca's mind when cannon roared from within the legation and he saw shots land in the vicinity of the palace.

The aim of cannon couldn't be adjusted as quickly as could rockets, but once the British gunners got their aim right their cannon would wreak havoc amongst Casca's rocketeers, and do much more damage to his palace than he could hope for his rockets to effect against the legation.

Casca gave some quick orders to Huang and, setting spurs to his horse, wheeled away from the action.

He found David Sen-yung obediently concealed behind a large warehouse with several hundred peasants. Sen-yung told him that other Boxer leaders had similar groups waiting for orders in various streets all around the legation.

Gritting his teeth at the thought of what he was doing, Casca ordered them to charge the legation and get into the grounds at all costs. He galloped away to issue the same orders to the other Boxer-led groups of peasants.

Meanwhile Huang was carrying out the orders Casca had issued him.

His infantrymen rushed to the walls with every available

ladder, rope, and grappling hook, placed them, and quickly retired to cover as the Boxers and their peasants arrived. Then the archers laid down a dense pattern of arrows, effectively keeping the British off the wall. And at the same time every possible rocket and fire dart was unleashed.

And into this rain of death Sen-yung and the other Boxers led their thousands of peasants.

Many of them fell victim to their own arrows and rocket fire, but most of them reached the walls and clambered up the ladders and ropes that the infantry had put in place.

Once on top of the walls the peasants were decimated by the machine-gun fire from within the legation; but, pressed from behind by the teeming horde, some of them made it into the grounds, and then some more, and then more.

The British machine-gunners had to divide their fire. Some of the big, clumsy guns were tilted down from firing at the walls to shoot directly at the peasants who were now on the ground charging at them. Lines of redcoats knelt in turn to fire their Enfield rifles into the peasants on the ground, too.

But, as fast as they fired, the British could not kill the Chinese as fast as they came over the walls.

And now and again a rocket from the palace took out a machine gun, or a group of redcoats—or a number of Chinese.

It made no difference. The storm of men could not be stopped. The Chinese eventually reached some of the British troops, and although the redcoats killed ten or twenty or more Chinese for every British soldier who fell, the peasants' farm and kitchen implements took their toll, and they tore apart the foreign devils with their billhooks, scythes, flails, and meat cleavers.

Now Casca nodded to Huang. Huang signaled, and his infantry came out from cover and charged in the wake of the dying peasants, using the mass of their bodies for cover once they reached the ground inside the legation. They advanced remorselessly on the machine gunners, then on the riflemen, and finally on the men at the cannons who were shelling the rocket stations in Casca's palace.

As Casca clambered over the wall he saw Huang, sword in hand, leaping into the grounds from another part of the wall.

Casca's archers were now getting established on the wall, and their big bows launched heavy three-foot arrows to devastating effect. Casca had joined these archers in practice, and had been astonished at the force of their six-foot bows. He estimated the required pull at two hundred pounds, more than twice the force of any other bow he had ever encountered.

From their vantage point on the wall the archers could pick their targets almost at leisure, and the long arrows thudded home repeatedly, rarely missing their man, and sometimes the one arrow passed clean through a man's body to skewer the man behind him.

With the wall secured, crossbowmen were able to take up position, some of them with chu-ko-nus, the repeating crossbows that could launch six bolts in a few seconds, and some with the very accurate pellet bows that fired clay balls or stones.

The chu-ko-nus wreaked havoc on the machine-gunners, and then on the cannon crews, as the crossbowmen could place each of the six successive arrows with increasing accuracy.

The Chinese soldiers around Casca rallied to their Hsia. A similar group formed around Huang and the two fought their way toward each other.

The British fought hard and well. Both officers and soldiers hated China and all Chinese, considered them barely human, and were always ready to butcher any number of them. But this action was like nothing they had ever experienced.

The numberless peasants had been bad enough, but now they were facing well-trained and well-led professional soldiers and were learning the hard way the uselessness of empty rifles. Hand-to-hand fighting was a form of warfare these men had never known, and they were no match for the sword-armed Chinese, who had never known any other battle mode.

Casca and Huang met, pausing to embrace. They held one whole corner of the legation forecourt. The British troops were now backed up against the legation building, a hundred or so redcoats in a square, the front ranks kneeling to fire their rifles, the next rank standing to fire theirs, and both these ranks retiring into the square to reload as they emptied their magazines.

There were a few machine guns in front of the square of British soldiers, and a lot more behind it on the legation steps, firing over the defenders' heads.

On the top steps, swords in hand, were the colonel of the legation guard and his senior officers. There were a few subaltern officers in the square and amongst the gunners, and the rest were with the hundred or so other redcoats who were defending the remaining three walls.

Alongside the colonel stood the British legate, a tall, spare figure, splendid in a royal blue tunis with gold epaulets, his gold-hilted sword disdainfully undrawn in its tassled scabbard, a cocked hat resplendent with ostrich feathers covering a fringe of thin gray hair.

It had not yet occurred to the British that they were losing, or that they could lose. And it made no difference. Surrender to a stinking horde of yellow animals was out of the question, and there was nowhere to run.

So the carnage continued.

Nobody thought of taking aim at the gorgeously arrayed figures of Casca and Huang. The British riflemen were trained to fire their guns and obey orders, not to think, and they poured their fire into the mass of the Chinese troops.

Nor did Casca's archers fire on the colonel and the legate, but they did concentrate their arrows on the machine-gun crews.

Each Maxim gun took five men to operate it. One man held the two handgrips and, as he squeezed the trigger, tried to point the bucking contraption in the general direction of the enemy. Another fed in the ammunition belt while on the other side a third pulled on the slack of the emptied belt to try to prevent it from jamming. In theory, the other two men were supposed to rush back and forth with fresh belts of ammunition and cans of water to cool the steaming mechanism. But, in practice, they laid prone, holding on to the tripod legs and trying to restrain the wild bucking of the gun every time the trigger was squeezed.

The gunners were easy meat for the archers. Any arrow that struck home temporarily immobilized the gun, no matter which man it hit.

Casca was charging a machine gun when one of the men holding it down was killed. The gun bucked wildly, snatching the belt from the loader's hands so that the belt jammed. The last round tore through Casca's chest and he went down.

As consciousness faded he saw Huang turn to look at him in consternation, then turn back to race again toward the gun.

His troops raced past him as Casca lay on his face, blood pouring onto the ground, the blessed relief of shock washing out the searing agony of smashed ribs and torn muscles. The bullet had passed through his right lung and out through his back, and Casca was drowning in his own blood, sinking into waves of darkness.

CHAPTER TWENTY

The blades of grass before Casca's eyes swam back into focus. He vomited a bucket of blood and felt the hideous wrench as the shattered bones of his ribs began to reknit.

The pain-twisted face of the Jew on the cross swam before his eyes as the bleeding slowed.

He rolled over onto his back to get his nose out of his vomit, and felt a gentle hand inside his armor. The face he saw was now Chinese, and as the needle went into his chest he recognized Poon Fong.

Then there was a long moment of absolute peace and ease.

The moment ended all too quickly, and Casca was staring up into the sun. Alongside him he could see Poon Fong bending over another wounded soldier. The pain in his chest was frightful, but he knew that the worst was over, that the curse of the Nazarene had once more taken effect. He was going to live, all right.

Fuck it. He was going to live forever.

His sword was on the ground beside him. He snatched it up and got to his feet in an insane rage.

Huang and some others had taken out the machine-gun crew and were now rushing the rifles.

Casca was alongside them in an instant, and together they fell upon the redcoats.

Casca's wrist shook as the downswing of his blade split a kneeling man's skull through to his neck. The force of his rush brought him chest to chest with the standing rifleman in the next rank, and the knife in his left hand disemboweled him while his sword arm swung in a flat arc to take off another man's head. Then he was upon the men who were squatting in the rear ranks to reload, their rifles lying useless in their laps as they hastened to change the five-round magazines.

It was like killing sheep in a pen.

One man managed to get his rifle up over his head, and Casca thought that either his sword or his wrist had broken as the force of his blow jarred his arm.

He furiously booted the squatting man in the throat, and hacked his belly clean open with his sword as he fell. Then he turned his wrist for the upswing, catching the next soldier between the legs, the slice continuing all the way up the red tunic till the point of the sword lifted him by the chin as it slit his throat.

Red blood sprayed all over Casca, and he shook it from his eyes as he hacked and slashed at everything that stood before him.

The square broke, the soldiers falling back in a wave to make a path for the blood-drenched horror with the iron face of a fiend from the very gates of hell.

Then Casca was fighting his way up the steps amongst the British officers. They fenced well, but none of them was any sort of match for the mindless, murdering monster that Casca had become.

Two captains and a major fell before his sword, and he dispatched the colonel with a single upthrust to the fat belly on the steps above him.

Still climbing the steps, he twisted his sword out of the

falling colonel's gut and was bringing it up to guard position when it was almost struck from his grasp.

He backed away crablike across the steps, and kept moving as a relentless rain of blows clashed steel against his steel.

The British legate had at last unsheathed his sword, and was flailing it at Casca with enormous energy and fantastic skill.

The whole of the rest of the battle vanished from Casca's awareness as he fought for his life.

For his part, the legate knew that he was the last Englishman between the Chinese and the women and children in the building, and he was determined to hold them all off single-handed.

In two thousand years of sword fighting Casca had learned barely enough to keep his measure with this man, just managing to stay out of reach of the furious Britisher's sword, but unable to make a stand that put him within striking distance.

They fought the whole width of the broad steps, and then the legate was forcing Casca down the slope toward the backs of the last of the retreating redcoats. He had killed a dozen or more men coming up these steps, and now one lone old man was slamming him back toward where he had come from.

And the benefit was all to the legate. He took advantage of his superior position and pushed Casca one step at a time, Casca wasting energy as he tried to reach up at him, while being forced to yield step after step.

When Casca backed away rapidly the legate declined to fall for the ploy and only reached after him with the tip of his sword, keeping him engaged, but despite his fury, running the fight as it suited himself.

And when the legate again closed, he advanced down a step in time with a slash or a thrust so that Casca had to parry and retreat and could not get in position to return the attack.

Casca recognized that he had met a better swordsman than he had ever before encountered, even among the gladiators of the Circus Maximus.

"But, fuck it, I've died once today, and that's enough," he spat.

Instead of retreating yet another step, he bent his knees so that he was almost squatting, and then came up in riposte, turning his wrist to bring up his sword in a great underhand swipe, the whole force of his straightening legs and back behind it, the edge of his sword reaching to slash beneath the legate's guard and open his belly.

But the old man simply wasn't there.

He had kept one foot on the upper step, and as Casca started his enormous slash he stepped up and away so that Casca's sword met empty air.

And then the legate's sword came down with all the fury of a man who was no longer fighting for a queen's empire, but for the lives of his own family.

His sword took Casca squarely in the face, the iron mask smashing his nose to pulp as it disintegrated into its several pieces.

Casca stood numbed by the blow.

Two steps above him the legate, too, stood still, momentarily shocked by the sight of a white face and blue eyes.

It was his last sight on this planet as Casca lunged automatically and buried half the length of his sword in the old man's gut, and the cocked hat and the elegant sword fell to the steps.

Casca allowed the falling body to slide off the length of his sword. He muttered as he surveyed the now-empty steps: "Thank all the gods there are no more like you."

He briefly saluted the crumpled blue tunic and raced

down the steps to the redcoats' backs, cleaving skulls, severing spines, lopping heads, and spitting kidneys as the startled troops found themselves squeezed between his sword and those of Huang and his men advancing up the steps.

In a few minutes there was not an Englishman alive on the steps.

Actually, there was scarcely an Englishman alive anywhere within the legation grounds. The thousand-strong Chinese soldiers who had stormed the walls with Casca and Huang had been followed by an even greater swarm of peasants, and these, together with the survivors of Senyung's attack force, were rampaging through the grounds, hacking and stabbing with their clumsy implements, even tearing at wounded redcoats with their bare hands until not a single foreign devil breathed.

And now they swept up the steps toward the great doors of the legation.

For a single instant Casca thought of trying to order them to desist, then he shrugged and turned away as they forced open the huge double-barred doors by sheer weight of numbers.

Scream followed terrible scream as the English women were raped and mutilated and their children torn apart by the frenzied mob.

Casca sheathed his sword and walked slowly down the steps and across the forecourt and out into the street to where his ostler stood patiently holding his horse.

Wearily he climbed into the saddle; he sat there while the horse slowly found its own way back to his palace.

CHAPTER TWENTY-ONE

Five days passed, and the city remained at a standstill, the normally placid Chinese peasants shocked out of their wits at their own monstrousness.

After the sack of the British legation the mob had turned its fury on the smaller and less-protected legations of all the other foreign powers. And on their churches, missions, monasteries, nunneries, schools, hospitals, orphanages.

By the third day there was not a live European to be found in the entire city. Nor were there many who had died easily.

The troops defending the legations had been smothered by endless numbers of Chinese who poured relentlessly over their lightly defended walls, ignoring the bullets and bayonets that killed them in their thousands till they came to grips with the foreign devils. The European and American soldiers and diplomats and businessmen and their families had been cut to pieces—often one piece at a time with kitchen knives—disemboweled, castrated, mutilated, their women raped, their children butchered.

Casca had stayed in his palace throughout the massacre, keeping his troops within the palace grounds, exercising and training them for the inevitable reprisals that he realized must come soon.

The British navy, Casca well knew, had more than three hundred ships of the line, and Britain launched more than a thousand new merchant ships each year. And he also knew too well that the British would sail every one of those ships up the Han River to Tsungkow if necessary to avenge the legation and to reinstate Victoria's rule.

The news that came to his palace from around the country was almost all bad.

The uprising had been almost entirely abortive, ill conceived, not at all planned, and badly led. The faith of the Boxers in their newfound philosophy compounded from the Bible, Paine, Marx, and Queensberry had been profoundly ill placed. And the faith of the peasants in the leadership of these crazy young men had served them very badly.

The uprising had, as expected, erupted throughout the entire country, but Tsungkow was one of the few places where it had met with any success. In other cities and county seats the foreign legations had been attacked and hundreds of Europeans and Americans had been massacred. But tens of thousands of Chinese had died in the event, and within a few days the rebellion had faltered to a standstill, the peasants sated with blood and disgusted with themselves, their Boxer leaders fighting amongst themselves, or simply having no idea what to do once they were in command of a village or town.

Worst of all, none of the expected support had materialized. The Freemasons had turned their backs on the rebels. Businessmen like Mr. Song had not even provided the expected money and arms. Sun Yat-sen and his Kuomintang Democrats had quite ignored the events. And the emperor and almost all of the imperial nobles had sided with the British and the other foreign devils.

In Chaochow, Baron Ying had ruthlessly put down the rebellion at first light on the first day of the new year, and,

Sen-yung's messengers warned, was even now moving against Tsungkow without waiting for the British to make it up the river from Swatow.

Casca sat at ease on the raised inner wall of his palace with Liang Yongming massaging his feet while he watched Huang Chu exercising troops for the coming battle.

Defeat was virtually certain, but Casca intended to make the best possible fight of it. The only hope of minimizing the reprisals was to reduce the number of able-bodied troops who could exact them.

A much-chastened David Sen-yung sat beside Casca. Despite his best efforts, he had failed to die in the attack on the legation and had been forced to swallow the bitter fruit of his dreams. Yet still he dreamed.

At every piece of good news of the rebellion he waxed enthusiastic once more. In Shanghai, Sian, Chengtu, and a number of other cities the Boxers had succeeded—to some degree. In Kwangtung, Szechwan, and even in the capital, Peking, many of the top Manchu officials had been assassinated. And in Nanking the Boxers had declared a provisional government independent of the Manchu emperor. The local Boxer leader declared that henceforth Chinese would create their own modern civilization, promote a peaceful life, and ensure that China would never again be a subdued nation.

"Fine sentiments," Casca grunted when Sen-yung read a copy of the proclamation. "There's a familiar ring to them."

But from other cities there came very bad news. Yangchow, once one of China's oldest and most important cities, had almost been completely destroyed in the British counterattack with the loss of tens of thousands of lives. A special tragedy, as the city had only recently been rebuilt, having been destroyed in the Taiping Rebellion just thirty-five years earlier.

Casca and Huang had put the five days to good use, and every soldier in every one of the city's numerous garrisons was on duty, living within the garrison with arms and armor close to hand. The smaller garrisons had forces of five to six thousand men under arms; some of the larger ones had twenty to twenty-five thousand. The men of all the garrisons had been divided into watches, and one third of them were standing by, ready for action at all hours. The remainder could be called upon within minutes.

Watchmen were on duty day and night in all the city's watchtowers, striking gongs every hour from sunrise to sunrise as water clocks measured out the time.

Trenches and holes for marksmen had been dug all around the outer perimeter of the city and in every open space between the walls. Atop the walls, coal fires were set, ready to be lit, and nearby were vessels full of water, fire pots full of oil, and ingots of lead ready to be heated and poured upon attackers.

Just outside the outer city wall Casca had set up a number of ballistas, giant slings that could hurl missiles of around ten pounds for distances of a quarter of a mile.

But when it came, the attack held no element of surprise.

Baron Ying rode toward the city at the head of an army of forty thousand men. In the late afternoon he encamped at a distance of a mile and sent ahead messengers demanding the surrender of the city and offering to spare Casca's life if he surrendered without a fight and gave up for execution David Sen-yung and all of the Boxer ringleaders, the Pao, the colonel of the city, and the leading elders.

Casca replied that none of these men was responsible for the sacking of the legations, and that he alone bore responsibility. He called upon Ying to withdraw his troops, warning him that if he failed to so do, he would attack his camp at dawn.

There was no reply from the baron, and on the stroke of

midnight Casca unleashed upon his camp a massive barrage of rockets fired from the palace, accompanied by several thousand agny astras, the fire darts being launched upon Ying's tents by troops who had crept to within a hundred or so yards under cover of darkness.

Hundreds of tents caught fire, and their occupants were milling around in confusion when Casca's archers opened fire on them and his swordsmen waded into them.

Ying's men had no chance. Few of them were within reach of their arms, the cavalry's horses had been driven off, and most of them had no choice but to flee.

Ying appeared, raging, and tried desperately to rally his men, but to little effect. By the time the sun started to light the sky the bodies of thousands of his warriors littered the field, and thousands more were in full flight.

Full dawn revealed that Casca had won, and at almost no cost to his own forces.

From the palace walls Casca and Huang saw the result, but did not bother to congratulate each other. They knew well that the real danger did not come from Ying's primitively armed Chinese troops.

The watchmen in the towers had barely started to sound the alarm when cannonballs started to fall upon the city and the palace.

Six British ships lay in the river, broadside on to the city, their banks of cannon belching fire and round shot. The British commodore had sailed his ships upstream to within a few miles of the city, then waited for darkness and launched longboats, the rowing crews towing the ships into place in the dark.

Casca had expected some such tactic, but the tables were nonetheless nicely turned on him. The cannonfire demolished whole buildings, including some of the garrisons, throwing the townspeople and the soldiers into panic. The British sailors knew exactly what they were doing, placing their shots about the city where they had the most telling effect.

Casca had a mental image of the British officers on their gun decks, working with detailed maps of the city that they had been preparing for years against just such an occasion.

Then the guns started firing chain and grape shot into the garrisons and the surrounding streets, cutting the surprised Chinese soldiers and the terrified citizenry to pieces, turning panic into rout.

Marines poured ashore from the ships and advanced in lines, firing as they marched, pausing to reload while the next rank leapfrogged, and then the next, maintaining a continuous fusillade that killed all before it.

Huang Chu managed to get some of his troops into order and his captains made stands here and there, but the archers were no match for the British rifles. The swordsmen could get nowhere near them, and the Chinese were forced to retreat continually.

And when the British troops came to open spaces like the city squares and the temple grounds or long stretches of straight street, they were able to set up their Maxim guns, and the Chinese were cut to shreds.

Street by street and corner by corner they advanced. Here and there Huang's men made determined stands, but to little avail.

The rocket crews turned their racks to face the river, and when they had adjusted their aim, scored a number of hits on the ships, setting fire to two of them, and igniting one powder magazine so that one whole ship exploded.

But in the narrow, twisting streets the rockets could not be brought to bear on the marines who advanced relentlessly, their rifles clearing street after street, the machine guns adding to the slaughter.

From the palace walls Casca watched. It was worse than

he had feared. His archers accounted for only a few of the riflemen, while the advancing Enfields and machine guns killed soldiers and civilians indiscriminately in enormous numbers.

And the British cannoneers quickly got the range of the rocket launchers and put them out of action in quick succession.

Then the marines were at the outer city walls, the defenders at last able to take some toll on their numbers. But once the machine guns were set up, the defenders on the walls were quickly wiped out.

Boiling water and lead and exploding clay pots full of burning oil rained down upon the attackers, but most of them stayed out of range and waited for the Maxims to wipe the defenders from the walls.

Chanting sailors came dragging small cannon along the streets to within a hundred yards of the outer walls of the city, and the huge wooden gates disappeared in a fiery mess of splintered wood and bleeding bodies.

The marines rushed through the gap and established a square of riflemen, and then a machine-gun crew set up inside the gates and swept hot lead about the space to the second wall.

When the cannon blew away the second set of gates, Casca wearily buckled on his sword belt, picked up his mace, and started down from the wall.

As he reached the ground he turned for a last look at his palace. Huang Chu, he knew, would die in the battle or be executed after it. His faithful Pao and the city elders would likewise be executed as an example to those in other cities. David Sen-yung had rushed out into the streets at the first cannonade and had probably thrown away his life.

Casca had said good-bye to all his concubines the previous night, and tenderly to Liang Yongming that morning. He raised one hand to wave farewell to his palace and his reign as Hsia.

CHAPTER TWENTY-TWO

"And where might the killer of Christ be going?" The woman's voice startled him and he turned to see the diminutive nun who had lashed him with her feather duster and with her tongue.

"Where the hell did you come from?" Casca laughed. He was actually pleased to see that the demented old fanatic had survived the slaughter.

Sister Martina laughed, too.

"Oh, I know this palace better than you do. Better than even the Pao, or Tian, or any of the team of concubines that you disgrace yourself with.

"This palace was first built in 635 A.D., during the T'ang dynasty. The T'ang dynasty granted refuge to Nestorian Christians who were being persecuted elsewhere as heretics—which they were and are. Around the tenth century they were persecuted again, and again in the sixteenth century, then in the eighteenth and nineteenth centuries, and now in the twentieth century.

"But Christianity has survived here, and one day all of China will be Christian—as you will surely live to see."

Casca grimaced. "Even your Messiah didn't curse me to live that long."

The nun was unperturbed. "We can afford to be patient.

It is written that all the world must be converted before the Second Coming.''

"Oh my God," Casca groaned.

"Don't blaspheme," the little nun snapped, and raised one tiny hand as if threatening a blow.

Casca laughed. "Where's your feather duster?"

"I didn't realize I would need it when I took refuge from the rioting.''

"Where did you find refuge?"

"Come, I will show you. Now you need refuge, and the Brotherhood of the Lamb must provide it for you. Loathe you as we do, we cannot afford to lose you.''

Casca turned away from her and headed for the sounds of battle in the outer courtyards.

"Good-bye, Sister. I don't need refuge, I need death.''

CHAPTER TWENTY-THREE

By the time Casca reached the outer wall of his palace, the British marines had broken through the last of the city wall defenses and were advancing on the palace.

Casca had selected from the palace stable the very best horse, a great black stallion with a great columnar neck, immense chest, and massive hindquarters. Its eyes were tinged with red, and it was perhaps a little mad—which suited Casca just fine. For what he had in mind he needed madness.

He galloped to the main gate in the outer wall of the palace where the palace guard were concentrated, prepared to sell their lives dearly.

"Fall back, fall back," he shouted, his arm waving the troops away from the gate.

The captain looked confused and worried, but passed on the order to his men, and they all withdrew to the left of the gate as Casca indicated.

"Open the gates. Quickly, quickly. Open all the gates."

The gatemen could not believe their ears, but they followed orders and cranked open the great gates just as the British sailors dragged a small cannon toward them.

The marines rushed through the opening and quickly

formed a square, the front ranks aiming at the retreating Chinese.

Casca raced around his troops like a crazed shepherd herding sheep.

"Retreat! Retreat! Fall back," he shouted, herding his men along the breadth of the open space between the first and second walls.

The subaltern gave the order, and the kneeling men emptied their magazines into the backs of the retreating Chinese.

Dozens of them fell, but most of them made it to the corner and escaped around it from the field of fire.

The young lieutenant was puzzled. The British had the whole broad field to themselves. He gestured with his sword and ordered an advance after the fleeing Chinese.

The marines hurried along the length of the wall, maintaining their square, wading through the streams and ornamental ponds until they reached the corner.

As they gained the corner another company appeared in the open gateway, just in time to see their comrades cut down by a fierce hail of arrows that took the square in its right flank.

The square turned and reformed, but most of the men who were now in the front rank had empty rifles and had not had time to reload in the pursuit of the fleeing Chinese. At the order to fire, the volley was ragged, and the next volley from the second rank was worse.

Then another hail of arrows fell upon the square, cutting down most of the men who had just emptied their rifles.

A new front rank formed, the kneeling men all with full magazines. But the Chinese were retreating again, and on the order to fire the marines emptied their guns into their backs. Many Chinese fell, but most made it to the protection of the next corner.

The new contingent of marines hurried to the assistance

of the first, reaching the first corner as the first group got to the next corner.

To be cut down again by hundreds of arrows.

The leading company was being drastically reduced in numbers. The British square was not designed for this sort of maneuver. Now the back rank was at the front, facing Casca's men with empty rifles. The few men who had reloaded were clumsily turning to their right, their own bodies impeding them in bringing their weapons to bear.

A third group of marines came through the gate and rushed after the others. The sailors were dragging their cannon through the gate, but with no clear idea of what they were to do with it.

Casca left his captain to continue the confusing maneuver and galloped right around the open space and back to the gate, now calling down fire from the men on the top of the walls, and shouting to the gatemen to close the gates.

Outside the walls two more contingents of marines came to a confused standstill. The cannon and most of their machine guns were now inside the closed gates, and the archers atop the wall were taking a heavy toll of them.

Casca ordered the next gates opened and led the first of his retreating troops through them into the next open space. The ragged square of marines was making its way back to the first gate, the speed of their advance preventing them from reloading, and the repeated right turns constantly bringing the wrong men into confrontation with Casca's men.

When they rushed through the second open gate the Chinese archers were waiting for them, and by the time they managed to regroup and reload the square had been almost wiped out.

Then it was the turn of the pursuing companies, and they fared no better. The subalterns in charge lacked battle experience, and nothing in their training had prepared them for this sort of fight. Nor could they see what was going wrong with the preceding contingent until it was happening to themselves.

The situation had now changed dramatically. The marines who had only half an hour before had the city at their mercy were now separated into five groups spread about the two open spaces while the defending Chinese were concentrated inside the second wall and on top of both walls.

The British cannon and Maxims had been rendered useless.

But their only orders were to attack, and they continued unprofitably to advance on the palace.

When Casca had the inner gates opened the trap was complete. Two contingents were outside the outer wall, their cannon inside the wall. They had some machine guns, but nobody to fire at.

The other three contingents were each alone in the space between two walls, and only the first one was in contact with the enemy on the ground, and were hugely outnumbered and disorganized.

Casca led an attack, racing his horse around the square to get to the men who were trying to reload, while his infantry overwhelmed the others by sheer weight of numbers.

The swordsmen cut the square to bloody pieces. Casca had the gates opened and they poured out to fall upon the second group with the same result.

And all the time the marines were subjected to the fire from the archers on the walls, while the heavy, clumsy Maxim guns had nobody to fire at.

Now Casca shouted for the main gate to be reopened and charged through it at the head of his infantry, sword in one hand, mace in the other, accounting for a British soldier with almost every swing of his arm.

More marines were now advancing from the river, but

the very speed of their unimpeded advance rendered them ineffective.

Inside the walls some of the Maxim crews had at last got their guns ready for action, but in one direction marines were retreating from the concentrated counterattack of the Chinese, and in the other direction were the newly advancing marines.

Casca, it seemed, had carried the day.

It seemed.

But he had not reckoned with Baron Ying.

The baron had regrouped what was left of his force and marched back to join in the British attack.

Now he was riding into the city at the head of the advance guard.

"Well, fuck it," Casca cursed, "I'm not really cut out to be a count anyway."

He broke away from the action and spurred his horse toward the baron.

"Fucking nobles," he fumed as he rode, "never do give the loyalty they demand. If he would join me I could push the British into the sea."

He drew his Webley and fired as he closed with the baron.

But the light bullet bounced harmlessly off Ying's shield. A second shot fared no better, glancing off his body armor. The third struck the chamfron that protected his horse's head, and another the poitrel on its chest.

Then he was busy using his shield to parry a lance thrust from the baron. They raced past each other and wheeled to meet again.

Casca aimed the Webley for Ying's chest as the baron drew from his holster his enormous handgun, slowing his horse as he held the four-foot length in both hands.

Casca's last bullet took him in the heart, but at the same

instant the huge ball from the baron's gun smashed its way through Casca's chest armor, splintering his ribs, punching a hole in his heart, and exiting through his back.

His mind screamed, *not again.* . . .

EPILOGUE

The marble felt cool and almost comfortable under his back. Two faces swam into focus and he recognized Sister Martina and the doctor Poon Fong.

All his weary mind could think was, here I am again. Will it never end?

Sister Martina smiled at him pleasantly as she raised the mallet above her head, saying gently, "I told you the Lamb would watch over you. You are not done with us yet. The rest may die and be in chains, but not you. You must be free." The smile changed. Years of cruelty washed over her face; the eyes grew narrow as spittle gathered into a froth at the corners of her mouth.

"Yes, you shall be free, though you deserve all the pain of the ages to be burned into your black Christ-killing soul. You should die ten thousand times for your sins. But you shall go free. We shall take you away from this land. There is no place for you here any longer!"

The mallet swung down, taking Casca away. Before the black claimed him he wondered where he would awaken this time, and to what?